DATE DUE

color blind

color blind

SHEILA SOBEL

MeritPress | fw

Published by
Merit Press
an imprint of F+W Media, Inc.
10151 Carver Road, Suite 200
Blue Ash, OH 45242. U.S.A.
www.meritpressbooks.com

ISBN 10: 1-4405-9746-4
ISBN 13: 978-1-4405-9746-6
eISBN 10: 1-4405-9747-2
eISBN 13: 978-1-4405-9747-3

Printed in the United States of America.

10 9 8 7 6 5 4 3 2 1

This is a work of fiction. Names, characters, corporations, institutions, organizations,
events, or locales in this novel are either the product of the author's imagination or, if
real, used fictitiously. The resemblance of any character to actual persons (living or dead)
is entirely coincidental.

Many of the designations used by manufacturers and sellers to distinguish their products
are claimed as trademarks. Where those designations appear in this book and F+W
Media, Inc. was aware of a trademark claim, the designations have been printed with
initial capital letters.

Women and New Orleans: A History by Mary Gehman and Nancy Ries, published by
Margaret Media, Inc., copyright © 1985, 1988, 1994, 1996, 2004. Sixth Printing. All
rights reserved. (www.margaretmedia.com)
Referenced with permission of publisher.

The New Orleans Voodoo Handbook by Kenaz Filan, published by Inner Traditions International
and Bear & Company, copyright © 2011. All rights reserved. (www.Innertraditions.com)
Referenced with permission of publisher.

Cover design by Stephanie Hannus.
Cover image © iStockphoto.com/itskatjas.

This book is available at quantity discounts for bulk purchases.
For information, please call 1-800-289-0963.

Dedication

For Michael

Acknowledgments

My deepest gratitude to all who are with me on this journey:

Jacquelyn Mitchard—for believing in me.

Deb Stetson and Stephanie Kasheta—for your enthusiasm.

UCLA Extension Writers' Program and Laurel van der Linde—for showing me the way.

SCBWI, Lin Oliver and Stephen Mooser—for your foresight in creating an organization specifically for authors and illustrators of children's literature.

CBW-LA, Nutschell Anne Windsor—for your friendship and encouragement over the years.

The Magnificent Seven Plus One writers' group and fellow UCLA classmates David Mellon, Mary Lynne Raske, Margaret Tellez, Janine Pibal, Kristen Baum, Manisha Patel, and Jake Gerhardt. I could not have managed without your insightful critiques and collective sense of humor.

Amy Rabins and Sandy Rabins—for reminding me that life is too short and for giving me the necessary push away from a corporate life into a life of writing.

Tink Ten Eyck—for your never-ending support.

Jason Dravis, The Dravis Agency—for your patience and guidance throughout the process.

Joe Mozingo—for inspiring me to research my own family heritage as well as create a fictional one for April.

Jackson Messick and Ava Messick—for finding delight in the world of words.

Michael—my unicorn. You are indeed a rare breed.

Chapter One

There's a whole lot of nothing on the way to New Orleans. I hadn't seen any evidence of civilization since we left Montgomery. Too wired to sleep, too tired to read, I leaned back and gazed into the darkness that had become my life. What a difference a week makes. Yesterday, I was an ordinary seventeen-year-old with a father who loved me. Last week, I had no thought of imminent threat to my ordinary existence. That was yesterday. Everything changed in a heartbeat. Literally. Not mine, but my father's, the very last beat of his thirty-five-year-old heart. Who knew he had a heart condition? Not me, but then again I knew so little about my family history.

In that moment, I became an almost-orphan. I say almost because my mom has been MIA in the Middle East for over a year. She simply vanished. Nobody knew how, when, or where it happened. Out on recon one minute, gone the next. Poof! MIA? AWOL? Kidnapped? The military was stonewalling. It only seems like forever, but it was just an hour ago that I boarded this stupid bus, my pathetic luggage hidden away in a compartment below like a stowaway. Before handing me my one-way ticket and saying goodbye, Sam, my father's friend and lawyer, said he would take care of packing up the house and storing everything for me. He said he would send the balance of my things after I was settled, not that there was much to send.

I didn't know it took six hours and twenty-five minutes to get to New Orleans from Montgomery, Alabama. I never needed to know, I never wanted to know. The bus? Who takes the freakin' bus anymore? A poor man's red-eye.

I felt like Harry on the Knight Bus, only without the four-poster bed or the magic. At least I had a window and there wasn't anybody sitting next to me. Thankfully, I wouldn't have to endure the idle chatter of another displaced soul.

Besides me, there were only a few other losers on their way out of Montgomery. A man as old as the hills sat two rows ahead of me. He wheezed constantly and farted every thirty minutes; I could've set my watch by him. There was also a granny who had not stopped knitting since she sat down. She must have a plus size sweater done by now or at the very least a dozen mittens. God help her if she dropped one of those needles—I was liable to use it as a weapon either on her or, perhaps, myself. The burned-out bus driver? Probably an ex-con who lied on his job application, trading in his orange prison jumpsuit for a gray one.

By now I was pretty sure I'd been dropped into some sort of geriatric Final Destination movie in glaring 3D. But where was the really hunky guy with the oh-so-stylish stubble who would come to save my day? With my luck, the hunky guy would save Granny because he has mommy issues.

What's next for me? An aunt I've never met, life in a city I've never been to, and, last but not least, yet another school in an endless parade of schools. Too bad Dad hadn't waited to die until next year after I'd graduated from high school.

Oh, man, I didn't mean that, Dad! If you're listening in, I hope you're up there watching over me. I need you; I miss you so much.

I started to well up but stopped, dabbed at my eyes with my sleeve. No, no tears. *Don't be such a baby.*

The knitting needles click-clacked in sync with the tires slapping the pavement; the large engine thrummed as the behemoth lumbered closer to New Orleans. The white noise finally worked its magic and I fell into a deep, dreamless sleep. Exhaustion was victorious in the battle with my anxiety.

I awoke several hours later as a red dawn was breaking over the horizon. My father always said, "Red sky in the morning, sailors, take warning!" I couldn't imagine how my life could get any worse than it already was.

As we neared the station, the bus rumbled through a disturbingly desolate neighborhood—a cement-colored urban landscape with little green for relief. No sign of life so early in the morning, only grayness and empty buildings.

Arriving on schedule at 5:30 A.M., the bus rolled to a stop. The hot engine tick-tick-ticked as the door whooshed open and the driver mumbled, "Welcome to New Orleans. Thank you for choosing Greyhound."

Like I had a choice, I thought, descending the stairs after the other passengers. I'd just spent six hours and twenty-five minutes in over-chilled, recycled bus air, and the June Louisiana heat and humidity dealt me a knockout blow. *Perfect. Just perfect.*

I hustled inside and scanned the cavernous station. I saw a woman who looked vaguely like my mother, but was smaller, with more curves and short, spiked hair.

"And so it begins," I grumbled to no one in particular as I walked towards my new life.

Chapter Two

"April?"

"Kate?"

We eyed each other warily, silently.

"Breakfast or sleep?" asked Kate.

"Breakfast."

Kate reached down. "Here, let me help you with your bags."

"I got it," I said, slinging my backpack over my shoulder and grabbing both bags.

"Alrighty then. We're over there," said Kate, pointing to a cherry-red Mini Cooper convertible. "Bacon and eggs? Vegetarian? What would you like?"

I threw my bags into the back of the car and got in.

"I don't care."

"Restaurant or home cooked?"

"I don't care."

"Home cooked, then. I'm a pretty good chef, you know."

"I don't know anything about you."

Filled with an uncomfortable silence, the little car sailed through the deserted city towards the French Quarter. At this hour, only the sidewalk cleaners occupied the streets, their hoses snaking behind them like alien pets.

"I'm sorry about your dad."

"Thanks."

"It must have been such a shock."

"I don't want to talk about it."

"Of course, I understand."

"I doubt it."

More silence.

"Are those your only bags? Is there more stuff on the way? Can I help you in any way?"

"Only two bags. The rest of my stuff will be sent. I don't need any help."

"Is there much? I can clear out some other things and put them in storage if you need more space."

"Not much."

"Do you need any money? I have some saved up if you need help."

"I'm good."

"Sounds like you're all set . . . Um, have you heard anything new from the Army? Are they any closer to finding your mother?"

"Stop the inquisition already."

I turned away from Kate and looked out the window, watching as the lifeless business district slipped away behind us, replaced by multicolored buildings with lacy wrought iron balconies. The delicate railings provided a brilliant backdrop for the vivid pinks and purples of bougainvillea and the dazzling green of cascading ferns. We wound our way past the river and through the narrow streets until at last Kate guided her tiny car into a parking space.

"This is it," she said, taking one of my bags.

I stopped at the gate, taking in my new home. The two-story yellow house was old, at least a hundred years. It was nice, but looked big for just one person; a storybook kind of house, except the fence was black wrought iron instead of white picket. The wraparound porch was furnished with white wicker rocking chairs, matching tables, potted palms, and several ceiling fans. A second story balcony, dripping tendrils of a lush green plant, had a set of French doors leading out from one of the rooms, probably Kate's bedroom or office, as there was only one white wicker rocker and a table.

Kate opened the door, "Coming?"

I picked up my backpack, reached for the other bag, trudged up the brick walkway and followed her inside.

Kate left her keys and handbag on a marble-topped antique hall table and headed up the stairs. I followed.

"I hope you'll be comfortable here . . . You'll have your mother's old room."

"Seriously?"

"This house has been in the family since my great-grandfather, but not to worry, it's been brought into this century for the most part. I have Wi-Fi and satellite television. I even have indoor plumbing! Let's get your bags put away, then I'll go start breakfast. Last one on the right. Your room connects to my office with a bathroom, but it's all yours, I have my own. I've emptied the armoire and the dresser for you."

"Was that my mother's?" I asked, looking at the four-poster bed.

"Yes, and it was our grandmother's before her. Most of the furniture in the house has been here forever. The mattress is new, though. By the way, you lived in this very room for a brief period, before . . ." Kate lowered her eyes.

"You mean *before* she abandoned me?"

Kate ignored my remark and pointed towards the bathroom, "There are clean towels if you want to freshen up. I'll go rustle up some breakfast." She turned to go, but stopped at the door. "Welcome home, April. I hope you can be happy here." She closed the door behind her.

I left my bag by the armoire, tossed my backpack onto the bed, opened the window, and turned on the ceiling fan. I flopped down into a comfy overstuffed floral wingback chair. Tired, angry, confused, and maxed out, I closed my eyes and drifted off. A short while later there was a quiet rap at the door. The aroma of bacon and coffee wafted through the house; my stomach rumbled in anticipation.

"Breakfast is ready."

I rose, stretched out the kinks, and headed to the bathroom. I threw cold water on my face and fastened my unruly curls with a clip before heading downstairs. I was a mess. My clothes were damp, wrinkled, and beyond needing to be changed, but I didn't care, I was ravenous.

Kate's kitchen was straight out of one of those slick architectural design magazines, furnished with a combination of high-end stainless steel appliances, well-worn cookware, and at least one of everything from Williams-Sonoma. Twin ceiling fans drew air in from the window over the sink, cooling the room. Looking out the window into her private courtyard, I saw a wrought iron dining table with matching chairs and a fountain burbling at the back. I opened a door that led to a screened-in porch filled with white wicker and more potted plants.

"You must be starving," said Kate.

She had set her vintage table with fresh flowers and linen napkins held in place by engraved silver rings. Fresh biscuits, nestled in an antique silver biscuit server, had been placed near a crystal bowl filled with chunky strawberry jam and a plate of molded fleur-de-lis butter pats.

"Please sit," said Kate, sliding fluffy Denver omelets next to perfectly crisped bacon.

I sat, sipped my fresh-squeezed orange juice, and watched Kate.

"Do you always eat so formally?"

"Most of the time I do. It was the way I was brought up, though I rarely eat in the dining room. I prefer to eat in the kitchen. I enjoy the whole process; there's something visceral about the

food prep, the table prep, and the satisfaction of a good meal."
She patted her hips. "Maybe a little too much satisfaction," she
laughed. "Eat. Before it gets cold."

Kate poured two cups of coffee and joined me at the table,
handing me one of the steaming mugs.

"Tell me about yourself. I know so little about you."

"Well, whose fault is that?"

Kate shrugged her shoulders, "You're right. I could have made
an effort over the years, but didn't. Your mother and I aren't the
closest of siblings, in case you hadn't noticed."

"I noticed."

Kate studied my face. "You remind me a lot of Julia. You have
her eyes and those curls . . ."

"I'm *nothing* like her."

". . . and her temper," Kate continued. "She was just about your
age when she got pregnant; not much older when she disappeared.
Our parents never forgave her. According to them, her sort of
behavior just didn't happen in 'good' families."

"If yours was what was called a 'good' family, I'd sure hate to
see a bad one." I pushed my plate away.

Kate bristled, "I'm sorry your life has been so disrupted, but
that doesn't give you license to be rude."

"Disrupted? That's what you call it? Really? Clueless. You are
absolutely clueless."

Kate stiffened. Her face flamed. "Life sucks sometimes, April.
Deal with it. I did. Growing up was no picnic for me. You weren't
the only one my sister abandoned. I was only thirteen. I had to
live with the fallout from her bad behavior *all by myself*."

Now I stiffened, stared unblinking at Kate.

Kate matched my stare. "And now, here you are and once again,
I get to deal with the consequences of her conduct."

I wanted to bolt, but had no place to go; tears threatened to flow.

Kate scrutinized me and debated, but said nothing. She rose from the table, handed me a tissue and asked, "More coffee?"

I nodded and looked around the room. "How can you afford this place?"

"Inheritance. Dad left pretty much everything to me."

"So, they hated her to the bitter end." I wrapped my arms tightly around myself and slouched in the chair.

"Not completely. Dad set up a trust fund for you."

That got my attention. "I'm *rich*?"

"No. When you turn eighteen, you'll have enough money for college, maybe even a car."

"I never knew."

"Me neither, not until after Dad died."

"How did they die?"

"Mom had liver cancer; Dad died a year later from lung cancer. Too bad you'll never get to know them. Then again, you're probably better off."

"Why?"

"Let's just say they were good, God-fearing, churchgoing folks with strong opinions of right and wrong, who thought their morals were above reproach; forever judging others harshly, but never themselves."

"Self-righteous right-wingers from a red state. Perfect."

Kate's face darkened; she turned inward. "What my parents failed to come to grips with is that every family, especially the judgmental, ultra-conservative ones, always has a skeleton or two in their closet."

Chapter Three

"Skeletons? What skeletons?"

"Our deep, dark family secrets, things that were never discussed, not in front of the children or polite company. Secrets and lies, lies and secrets," answered Kate from a deep, dark place of her own.

"What are you hiding from me?" I stood quickly, the chair legs scraping the hardwood floor.

Kate snapped out of it, arched an eyebrow and stared at me. "I've said too much already."

"So, you're just going to leave me hanging?"

She loaded the last dish and closed the dishwasher. "Go unpack. Get settled in. Get some rest. You need it more than you realize."

"I can't rest. You loaded me up with too much caffeine," I accused.

"The coffee was decaf. If you let yourself unwind, even a little bit, you'll crash. Here's your house key and my cell and work numbers. I'll be back tonight around nine," said Kate, collecting her handbag, car keys, and chef's jacket.

"You're leaving me alone?"

"It's what you wanted isn't it?" Kate softened. "April, listen to me. You need time to process everything that's happened. Be nice to yourself. Take a shower. Take a nap. Read. Surf the Net. Do whatever you can to relax. I've gotta go."

I watched Kate drive away. Now what? Barely 9 A.M. and the house was already stifling. Kate had opened the windows and turned on the ceiling fans downstairs, but it wasn't helping. I looked around for an air conditioning control, found none. *Who updates a house and doesn't add central A/C? Lame, really lame.*

With nothing else to do, I wandered from one immaculate room to the next, checking out Kate's house. The living room, shaded by the porch, gave the appearance of being cooler than it was. The floor-to-ceiling walk-through windows were draped in a soft ivory fabric that matched the sofa and chairs. A gold-framed mirror over the fireplace added light to the room. Muted but expensive-looking antique rugs covered gleaming hardwood floors.

The absence of family photographs screamed issues.

I flipped the switch in the formal dining room. Soft light from a crystal chandelier danced in another gold-framed mirror over another fireplace. A polished mahogany table for eight, a matching marble-topped sideboard, silver candelabras, and vases with silk flowers filled the room. *No wonder she doesn't eat in here, it's as stiff as a funeral parlor.* I studied a small Impressionist painting hanging over the sideboard. The signature looked like *Renoir.* Judging from the rest of the house, I doubted it was a knock-off.

The house felt like old money. It also felt like . . . I couldn't quite describe it. *Empty? Staged?* Everything felt displayed, ready for its close-up. *Weird.* Either Kate didn't use any room besides the kitchen or she was OCD and couldn't live with anything out of order. Or maybe a little of both. I opened doors, snooped through the downstairs closets, found nothing out of the ordinary. A powder room off the entry hall had hand towels that were so flat and straight, I wondered if she ironed them.

Circling back to the kitchen, I opened a door to a butler's pantry. The glass-fronted cabinets held a collection of silver serving pieces and china dinnerware. A ring with a spare set of Kate's car key, house key, and a small flashlight hung from a hook by the light switch. In the sunroom, another ceiling fan drew air in through the screened windows; it was much cooler out here. A basket filled with cooking magazines sat next to the loveseat; no *People* or *Cosmopolitan* for Kate. This room was more comfortable, more inviting. I pictured Kate hanging out here, cozied up on the overstuffed sofa cushions reading her magazines, while something simmered on the stove.

In the private courtyard, bright green grass peeked out between the uneven, worn bricks of the centuries-old floor and dark green ivy crept up the high brick walls. A single, large magnolia tree sheltered the entire area. I could feel history here in the quiet solitude of this, this . . . sanctuary. I didn't know what else to call it. It was so beautiful, so serene. Except for the addition of brightly colored cushions on the ancient black wrought iron furniture, nothing had changed here for a very long time. I felt oddly comforted and sat, decompressing, until the tiredness hit me like an oncoming Metro car. It was way beyond time to go lie down.

I took a bottle of water from the fridge and climbed the stairs to my room. It didn't take long to unpack my stuff. I slid the suitcases under the bed, removed my laptop from the backpack and plugged it in to charge, ditto my phone. I flopped down on the bed and watched the ceiling fan spin. If I hadn't been in such a foul mood, I would've thought this was a pretty nice bedroom. I'd never had a room this elegant before. It was a tasteful, feminine room with antique mahogany furniture, pastel floral fabrics, and white lace draping the windows and the four-poster bed. There was no trace of its former occupant, which, for some reason, made me sad.

I tried to picture my mother growing up in this room. *What kind of toys did she have as a little girl? Did she have posters on the wall when she got older? Did she study herself in the mirror, playing with hairstyles or trying out new dance steps? Did she have a phone of her own, or a television?*

What was she like as a pregnant teenager in this room, in this bed, at my age, with me on the way? Folding my hands over my own abdomen, I wondered what life was really like for her. *Was she happy? Was she angry? Was she frightened? Did she love my father? Was I nothing more than a mistake? Am I the booby prize in a contest between raging hormones and religious beliefs? I never got the full story from either my father or my mother. They always said we would talk about it when I got older, when I was better equipped to understand. What a load of nonsense. Now it's too late. I will never understand her. I will never forgive her.*

Long-buried resentment surged through my soul, threatening to sink me even further than I already was. I shut my eyes to the pain and before long, fell into a deep, fitful sleep. Skeletons laughing and singing *"Secrets and lies, lies and secrets"* danced in my head. I slept the sleep of the miserable, tossing, turning, tossing some more.

Around half past five, I awoke disoriented, drenched in sweat, desperately thirsty, and with a pounding headache. I reached for the bottle of water. It was warm, almost hot; barely drinkable. The air was so thick with humidity, I couldn't breathe. I needed to get out of the house. Thirty minutes and a stinging cold shower later, I dressed in loose clothing, slipped into my sandals and headed out the door. At the gate, I stopped dead in my tracks. Where on earth was I going? I didn't even know where I was. Right or left? Left or right? I decided to follow a group of tourists passing in front of Kate's house.

I shadowed the tour group as they made their way up Royal Street. I tried to pay attention to my surroundings, noting street signs as we shuffled along. I needed to be able to find my way back before Kate got home. The group halted at a small Victorian-style hotel surrounded by a cornstalk wrought iron fence. As the out-of-towners snapped their photos, the guide gathered everyone close and began to weave her story.

"The Cornstalk Hotel was built in 1816 as the home of our first Chief Justice of the Louisiana Supreme Court 'n' author of the first history of Louisiana, Judge Francois Xavier-Martin.

"Later on, Harriet Beecher Stowe, a guest at the house, was inspired to write *Uncle Tom's Cabin* after seein' the nearby slave markets. In 1840, the home's new owner added the cornstalk fence as a gift for his homesick wife who wanted to return to Iowa. Isn't that just the most romantic thing?" she giggled.

"One of the most notable things about this bed-and-breakfast are the ghosts of the children who haunt the hallways. They can be heard laughin' and runnin' up 'n' down the stairs, all around the hotel. They love cameras, so don't be afraid when y'all look at your pictures, 'cause you may not be the only ones waving in the photographs!"

There were light murmurings as the crowd moved away from the hotel, some inspecting their digital displays looking for ghostly children, like what the guide said was actually real.

Must be a haunted history tour, I thought as I trailed behind, pretending to window shop, since I hadn't paid to join the tour.

Everyone stopped again. The guide continued, "Here we are at one of our most haunted houses, the Lalaurie House, formerly owned by the high society couple, Dr. Louis Lalaurie 'n' his lovely wife, Delphine. Once celebrated for their grand balls and charitable work, the dark side of their souls came to light after a fire broke out in their home. Behind a locked door on the third floor, firemen discovered a number of dead or dying slaves, many of whom had been used in the doctor's experiments. It is believed that the cook, who they kept chained to her stove, started the fire. In the midst of the chaos, the good doctor and his wife escaped into the night, never to be heard from again."

"Chained to the stove?" said one of the group as we moved away from the building.

"Our final stop tonight is the Hotel Monteleone, where dozens of former guests and employees are rumored to have taken up residence for all eternity. If any of y'all are staying here, think twice about opening your door tonight, it might not be room service that's come a knockin' . . . Thank you kindly for joining me this evening for a tour of this great haunted city of mine. Now go on in and check out the hotel bar, the Carousel. Get yourself a Hurricane or Sazerac or something to settle your jangled nerves."

My stomach rumbled; I was famished, it had been a long time since breakfast. Up ahead, a cafe advertised soups and sandwiches. I broke away from the group and went inside.

Chapter Four

The café was empty, except for a heavily tattooed waitress and the short-order cook. I took a table near the window and watched as a young, skinny musician dressed in black set up his street corner stage. He plugged in his speaker, hooked up his violin, lay down his case for tips, and began to play something jumpy. Cajun? He was quite talented. Soon a crowd gathered around, clapping and tapping their feet to the rhythm. I heard the clink of coins as tips dropped into the case.

"What can I get for you, hon?"

I read the chalkboard menu. The special sandwich of the day was "Oyster Po' Boy"; the very thought of it made me queasy. I ordered a turkey on wheat and some sweet tea. While waiting for my food, I listened to the music and watched the world go by, trying hard not to think about my life. But it was all I could think about.

Why did Dad have to die? Where is my mother? What does Kate mean by secrets and lies? What did I do to deserve any of this? What am I supposed to do now? Why can't I just have a normal life like every other teenager? Like maybe divorced parents, with me shuttling back and forth between homes every other weekend, each parent trying to win my affection by showering me with clothes, gifts, and too much freedom? Maybe even a dog? But noooo! I've been swept into this miserable life like Dorothy in the tornado.

I've heard that children choose their parents before they are born. If that's true, what could I possibly have been thinking?

23

What's next for me? Who knew? Whatever it is, I doubted it would be good.

My head was spinning. I searched my bag for aspirin and took two. Like my favorite movie heroine, Scarlett O'Hara, I'd think about it tomorrow.

My food was served quickly; I dove in. Food and music—it was exactly what I needed. After another glass of sweet tea, with enough sugar to over-amp anyone, I paid my tab and headed up Royal Street, but not before tipping the hardworking, talented street musician.

Since I didn't know New Orleans at all and had no particular destination in mind, I just walked. I passed the police station, noticed a crowd gathering in front of a place called Café Beignet. Everyone was talking excitedly about the Voodoo and Cemetery Tour that started soon. With no real thought, I bought a ticket, took a brochure, and got in line to wait for the tour bus. Cemeteries and Voodoo temples suited me just fine. *I'll just go look at someone else's skeletons for a while.*

The van rolled to a stop. The doors opened. A tall, hunky young guy with his oh-so-stylish stubble appeared in the doorway. When his gaze fell on me, I stopped breathing. One hand flew to my head to try to smooth down my frizzy curls, the other hand worked to straighten my clingy skirt. Darned humidity!

He came down the steps, smiled warmly, and greeted the tourists—"How're y'all doin' tonight? Y'all ready to be spooked? I'm Miles, I'll be your guide this evenin' as we explore the dark history of N'awlins"—his accent a little bit of France and a little bit of . . . Brooklyn? "Now, if y'all can't understand somethin' I say, let me know and I'll repeat. I never knew I had an accent until some Yankees complained they couldn't understand a word I said. Imagine that!" He laughed. "I speak Yat, a dialect born from the melting pot of Europeans which settled this great city.

"We'll be headin' out to Saint Louis Cemetery Number One, Congo Square, and Magique et Medecine, a Voodoo emporium and apothecary. Anyone here know anythin' about our cemeteries or our Voodoo?" he asked. Nobody raised a hand.

"Okay, then, let's get started. All aboard! Watch your step, now, heah?"

Miles collected the tickets while everyone settled in, their cameras at the ready. I took an empty seat by a window at the back of the bus and watched Miles watching me in the rearview mirror. He smiled and winked. With a whoosh, the door closed and the van rolled away from the curb.

Miles began his spiel. "Saint Louis Cemetery Number One is the oldest and most famous of the New Orleans cemeteries, opening for business in 1789. Today, the cemetery is no longer open to the general public, it is open only for tours or to family members who own tombs. Spanning one square block and housing over 10,000 deceased, it is truly a city of the dead. The dearly departed are entombed in above-ground vaults, either because of the high water table of N'awlins or the traditions of the French and Spanish settlers. Now y'all pay attention. This is not a place to wander about alone! When we arrive, DO NOT stray from the group."

Miles continued, "Many famous Louisiana folks are buried in Number One. Probably our most famous resident of Number One is Marie Laveau, the infamous high priestess of Voodoo. She's interred in the Glapion family crypt, along with many of her fifteen children. Legend has it, if you mark her tomb with three Xs made from a soft brick she will either grant your desire or come to visit you in your dreams with solutions to your problems, after which you are to return to her tomb with an offerin' for her spirit. Does anyone have any desires they want granted tonight?" Miles grinned, looking in the rearview mirror directly at me.

Miles had his audience, including me, spellbound. I listened and watched as he charmed and informed our tour group. He didn't look much older than me. No apparent piercings or tattoos, which worked for me. I wasn't big on tats. He was tall, dark, and handsome and if I had a "type," he would be it. Those dark eyes, the "come hither" look, the crooked grin, the whole package must work well on the ladies, both young and old. I was betting he had a huge tip jar.

The van slowed to a stop. "We have arrived!"

I looked out my window, stared into the cemetery, and was struck by the enormous city of the dead. There were hundreds of decaying crypts, a stark contrast to my father's manicured, evergreen final resting place. The tombs sat close together in a macabre urban sprawl, littered with broken walkways and dirt paths. A black cat ran stealthily past the open wrought iron gate. Was it really bad luck to have a black cat cross your path? I hoped not. No longer sure I'd done the right thing by taking this tour, I lingered in my seat while the rest of the group descended the stairs. Miles gave each guest a souvenir, a small red bag with the tour company information on its tag. He called it a gris-gris, a magic bag that should (but didn't guarantee to) keep us safe. I doubted a little bag would keep anyone safe in this frightful neighborhood.

Miles climbed aboard the van, handed one to me, and asked, "Are you okay?"

"Never better," I lied. "Let's go."

"Listen up, everyone! I'll guide you through the cemetery. However, please do be careful. The ground is uneven and the cracked sidewalks are a bit of a hazard. The ancient tree roots can sneak up on you if you aren't paying attention. Once again, we need to stay together. DO NOT wander from the group. This is a very dangerous place to be alone."

The group, not wanting to get separated in the evening shadows, drew closer together and moved as one behind Miles through the cemetery towards the Glapion family crypt.

Miles continued, "Marie Laveau was both a Catholic and a Voodoo queen, sometimes practicing her Voodoo rituals in the Saint Louis Cathedral. She was a free woman of color who worked as a hairdresser to the upper class. Many believed she was all powerful, that her spirit still is. She was someone to be feared, either because of her Voodoo practices or her political influence. Either way, there is no denyin', she left her mark on N'awlins society.

"Okay, everyone, let's explore a bit more before it gets too dark. Let's all go check out the pyramid mausoleum, built to be the final restin' place of the Hollywood superstar, Nicolas Cage."

The crowd, led by Miles, moved away without me. I knelt to inspect the offerings scattered in the dirt. Candles, flowers, neon-colored strands of Mardi Gras beads, handwritten notes; a variety of trinkets were left by believers in hope that the spirit of Marie Laveau would help rid them of their problems or, possibly, to hurt someone. Entranced, I touched the cool, rough surface of the ancient crypt, lightly tracing the Xs left by those seeking help. From somewhere deep within, Marie's energy pulled, compelling me to mark three Xs myself. I looked around for something to use, found a fragment of red chalk. Wild gusts of hot air whipped through the graveyard; gunmetal gray clouds gathered overhead, obscuring the rising moon. Chilled to the bone, I shivered in the silent cemetery, as if someone were dancing on my grave. Not sensing the presence behind me, I yelped when a hand grabbed my arm.

"Just curious, little lady—what did you not understand about getting separated from the group? Remember, dangerous? Bad neighborhood? Not alone? Any of that ring a bell?" Miles seemed genuinely concerned.

My heart was pounding. "I'm—I'm sorry, I didn't realize everyone had gone," I stammered, embarrassed.

"You gave me quite a fright when I realized you weren't with us," said Miles, annoyed. "I'm responsible for this group."

"I said I was sorry"—shaking his hand away, letting the chalk slip through my fingers. Now I was annoyed.

"Maybe if you're up to it after the tour, you can offer a proper apology over coffee?" he flirted.

"I'll think about it," I replied, knowing I wouldn't have to think too hard. Miles gently took my elbow and guided me safely back to the van.

Miles began again, "Congo Square, now a part of Louis Armstrong Park, was a Sunday meetin' place for slaves. Louisiana law forced slave owners to give their slaves a day off and a place to gather. Congo Square was the 'in' place to gather for Voodoo and drumming rituals. Sundays at the Square gave the slaves a sense of community and the freedom to practice their beliefs. The Sunday gatherin's also attracted crowds of curious white folks. Eventually, Sundays at the park grew into a day of performance art and entertainment.

"Congo Square was also close by Storyville, now the Iberville projects. That's the neighborhood we just left, over by the cemetery. You may have already heard Storyville was the birthplace of jazz. Many of our jazz greats got their start on Basin Street between Canal Street and Beauregard Square, but that's a whole other N'awlins tour, the Magical Musical History Tour!" laughed Miles.

"Our last stop in the French Quarter tonight will be a house of Voodoo magic and medicine. Devotees say that Voodoo is not based on either white magic or black magic, but on spiritual power and the art of healing. That being said, their focus is also on retail power. If you are so inclined, you'll be able to purchase CDs and videos of haunting Voodoo chants and rituals performed by world-renowned practitioners!" said Miles, bringing the van to a stop in front of the building.

The rest of the group disembarked, but I stopped to speak to Miles, "Back there, in the cemetery, you lost your accent. What's up with that?"

Miles grinned sheepishly. "The stronger the accent, the bigger the tips! I need money for my school books, car insurance, dates, so I ham it up a bit."

"A bit? There's enough ham in you to serve twelve people for Easter dinner!" I laughed. "Maybe you can tell me more over that coffee I owe you?"

I winked and went down the steps to explore the Voodoo emporium and apothecary.

Chapter Five

The group was nowhere to be seen. Looking back, I watched Miles in the van checking his cell phone. The streets were empty except for the tour van. The air was thick, heavy with humidity. The hot wind blowing through the trees stirred eerie shadows around the porch as wind chimes danced on a hook beneath the rafters. The floorboards creaked beneath my feet as I reached for the door-knob. I looked around, then up, startled to see a baby alligator head hanging over the doorway, its mouth gaping in eternal sur-prise. Smoky incense drifted out the door, swirling past me and into the night like a ghost. Rhythmic drumming and low moan-ing could be heard coming from somewhere in the night.

Nothing to be afraid of, right? I entered the dimly lit space. The front room was empty; my group had disappeared. The apothecary and emporium wasn't much more than an ancient two-story house converted into a tourist attraction. Mind you, it was a totally creepy tourist attraction. The tiny space was a black magic flea market crammed with items for sale. A clothesline full of blue, green, and yellow headscarves hung beneath the ceiling over display racks filled with stuff I'd never seen or even imagined.

Large apothecary jars, labeled with names I didn't recognize, contained dried herbs: Five Finger Grass, Black Snake Root, Dragon's Blood Reed, Devil's Bit. *Where do they come up with these names? What is this stuff?* Everything was organized into neat categories: Healing, Good Fortune, Love, Protection, and Psychic Development. *No doubt, I could use some good fortune in my life!*

Candles of all shapes, sizes, and colors filled an antique hutch, their uses described in graceful script on ivory note cards: white for spiritual strength, light blue for protection, red for love, and black for evil or mourning. *Should I buy some black ones? Couldn't hurt.*

Spell books, books of chants, hexes, white magic, black magic, reference books on women of color, and a number of how-to Voodoo books filled the shelves of a corner bookcase. No copy of *Voodoo for Dummies*, however.

A discreet sign indicated *Custom made gris-gris bags are available, inquire at the front register.* On the walls, tribal masks with empty eyes watched my every move. The overly warm, incense-laden gift shop was claustrophobic, suffocating. Feeling lightheaded, I stumbled through a gauzy curtain into the next room and, following the music, went out the back door.

My group sat circled around two dreadlocked men chanting and beating African drums near a flaming fire pit. *Is this the beginning of a Voodoo ceremony? Probably not, just a show for us tourists.* The small courtyard, enclosed by brick, was unkempt, weed-filled. The untended courtyard was the antithesis of Kate's perfect serenity garden. In the far corner was a cage full of chickens; opposite that, a pen with a young goat. *Chickens? Goat? In the city? What kind of place is this?*

I'd had enough. It was time to get back to the van. Heading through the back of the shop, I spotted a door barely hidden behind a large African wall hanging. I tried to open it, found it was locked. *I wonder what's inside.* I heard movement in the other room. I moved the curtain aside, spotted the source. A tall, elegant black woman stood behind a glass display cabinet filled with elaborate Voodoo dolls. She closed the cash register drawer, straightened a countertop arrangement of oils, CDs, and DVDs, and turned towards me.

"Welcome! How might I help you tonight?"

Haitian? Jamaican? South African? I couldn't peg her accent.

"Dunno."

"What is it you seek, my lady? Love or money?" She smiled, her pale gold eyes locked on mine. I couldn't move.

"Hmmmm. No, neither love, nor money. I see a great sadness in you, a great loss. You are suffering, are you not?" she asked, no longer smiling.

I looked away.

"Fate has brought you here to me tonight, Miss. I can help you, you know." Her silky smooth voice was hypnotic. "Would you like some tea?" she asked.

"No! I mean I can't. Thank you. I'm sorry. I have to get back on the bus."

"What is your hurry, my dear? The others are still outside enjoying the music. Follow me, I shall take you back to them."

I moved quickly towards the exit, stopped short when I glimpsed a glistening white python curled up on top of a tall display case, his tiny red eyes looking down on me. I hadn't seen him when I was exploring earlier. Hastily backing away, I slammed into a tall metal shelf. Hundreds of handmade Voodoo dolls rained down around me.

I screamed.

Everything went black.

Chapter Six

When I opened my eyes, Miles was hovering over me.

"Are you here to save my day?"

"Well, somebody had to and Superman wasn't available." Miles held out his hand to help me up. "You know, I've rescued you twice already this evening and I don't even know your name. You do have one, don't you?" asked Miles.

"April. My name is April," I mumbled, disoriented, still lying on the old wooden floor, covered in a pile of Voodoo dolls with my skirt hiked up indecently.

Perfect. Just perfect, April. Way to impress a guy. Definitely not a good omen.

I brushed away the Voodoo dolls, yanked at my skirt and tried to sit up. I looked up at the shelf where the snake had been. It was nowhere in sight. Maybe there hadn't even been a snake. Maybe with the heat and the incense and everything else, I had imagined it.

"I'm sorry for the mess. Did I break anything? Can I help you put the dolls back?" I asked the shopkeeper, who was kneeling beside me, muttering softly.

"Tomorrow, you come back for help, my lady," she replied quietly. "Goodnight to you."

In one swift movement, she was gone.

"What was that about?" asked Miles.

"I, uh, I guess she wants me to help her clean up tomorrow," I stammered, as Miles helped me to my feet.

"Everyone is back on the van except us. Are you ready to go?"

"More than ready. Let's get out of here."

The drive back to Café Beignet was mercifully uneventful. Miles had finished his commentary, and for that I was thankful. I let the air conditioning work its magic on me and felt semi-restored by the time the van rolled to a stop. While the older ladies exited the vehicle, they gushed and filled the tip jar, no clink of coins for Miles, only the soft rustle of countless bills. The husbands snapped final photos of Miles next to his van.

After emptying the tip jar into a money bag, Miles, looking pleased, followed me down the stairs, locking the van behind him.

"You know I'm going to take you home now, right?" asserted Miles.

"No."

"Yes."

"No!"

"Might I remind you that the tour lasted only ninety minutes, during which time, I rescued you twice. That's once every forty-five minutes," said Miles, looking at his watch. "You're due for another rescue in about twenty minutes. I should be there for it."

"Miles, you're very sweet, but I don't know you. Why would I let you walk me home?"

"How can you possibly say that after all we've been through together?" he asked, his dark eyes twinkling in the moonlight.

"It's easy."

"Tell you what, I'm an honorable man," he said, placing his hand over his heart. "I know someone in there who will vouch for my good character." Miles pointed to the police station.

"Who? One of the prisoners?"

"Oh, how you wound me! Please come with me. You owe me, remember?"

"I only owe you coffee and this place is closed." I tapped the sign in the window of the café.

Miles pointed to the police station again, "They have coffee in there."

"You're joking, right? The *police station*? Stale police station coffee? Don't you watch TV? The coffee is always old and cold!"

"Little lady, I do hope you're worth all this bother," said Miles. He took my elbow and guided me up the steps to the station.

"You'll have to stick around to find out."

It was just about 9:30. All was fairly quiet inside the police station. Everyone seemed to know Miles. They all winked, nodded, and whispered when we entered. I didn't know if that was a good thing or not. A mini-museum with display cases full of New Orleans Police Department historic artifacts fronted the main desk. We passed several vending machines full of NOPD souvenir tee shirts for sale. Miles led me through to a bullpen area, where the officers on duty were busy with the usual Saturday night array of drunk and disorderlies. We stopped at a desk littered with stacks of paper, an empty NOPD coffee mug, and a worn block of wood with a brass nameplate, *Detective Frank Baptiste*. A dark-haired, movie-star handsome, early-forties man looked up from his computer keyboard. He smiled blankly at us.

"What brings you here tonight?" he asked, rubbing the tiredness from his eyes.

"Sorry to disturb you, sir, but this little lady . . ."

"April. My name is April Lockhart."

". . . needs some assistance," answered Miles.

"Really, how so?" The detective looked directly at me.

Miles responded, "Well, sir, she needs to know that I am of good heart and sound character."

"She does, does she?" asked Detective Baptiste. "Why?"

"She won't let me take her home, since we just met and all," replied Miles.

"Smart girl. 'Stranger! Danger!' That's what we tell the kids on Safety Day at the schools. One can never be too careful these days, no matter your age. Tell you what, Miss April. I'm due for a break anyway. How 'bout you let me take you home?" asked the detective, rolling his chair away from the desk.

"Thank you, sir. I would appreciate it."

Detective Baptiste removed his gun from the drawer and slipped it into its holster. He straightened his tie, adjusted the badge on his belt and rolled the chair back under the desk.

"Are you coming with us, son?" he asked.

"Sure thing, Dad!"

I glared at Miles.

"He didn't tell you I was his father, did he? He does have a good heart and he is of sound character, but not always of sound mind! He must like you, though. He's never brought a girl to the station before."

"So, I should be flattered?" I laughed.

"Oh, you're a feisty one, aren't you? No apparent Southern charm."

"You find me lacking in charm?" I asked, mocking offense.

"I'd say you possess a different kind of charm, not like most of the girls he knows. You seem to be a tad more edgy than polite."

"Soooo, Miles has a lot of girlfriends?" I asked, curious.

"No, nobody special. He keeps himself too busy for girls, what with work, school, and all of his causes."

"Hellooooo! I'm right here," said Miles, lagging a few feet behind us.

We left the station and headed down Royal Street towards Kate's house. The wind gusted and whipped at my skirt. The moon disappeared again, the air changed; I could smell the coming rain.

All of the shops had long since closed for the night. The empty sidewalks were dark, dogs howled in the distance. I was grateful to have company.

The three of us approached the house, where lights illuminated almost every window. *Uh-oh.* When I left the house earlier, it was still daylight; I hadn't turned on any lamps. A scowling Kate stood on the porch, her arms folded tightly across her chest.

"Yikes, your mom doesn't look too happy," whispered Miles.

Chapter Seven

I agreed with Miles. Kate looked the opposite of happy.

"She's not my mother, she's my aunt," I whispered.

"Where have you been? No note. No voicemail. Nothing at all?" demanded Kate.

She sprinted down the steps towards me. "When I couldn't reach you, I got concerned. I was about to call the police."

"No need for that, ma'am. I am the police," said Detective Baptiste, revealing his badge.

"Police? What have you gotten yourself into, young lady?"

"Hold on, hold on. She's not in trouble, at least not with the police. She made a good judgment call. She asked for my help in getting home safely. Smart girl you have there."

She hesitated, "Well, um . . . okay, then. Thank you, Detective. Officer," said Kate, turning towards Miles.

"He's not a police officer, he's my son, Miles. Apparently, he's been working real hard this evening to impress Miss April here," he laughed. "I'm not so sure that it's going all that well, though. What do you think, ma'am?"

"Kate. My name is Kate Doucet. Pardon me, I forgot my manners. Would you like to come in? I can put on some coffee. I've got homemade cookies, cakes, pastries, too."

Lightning flashed, thunder rumbled in the distance; it started to drizzle.

"How 'bout we take a rain check? I need to get back to the station," he said, taking Miles's arm, turning him towards the gate.

"Wait!" said Miles. "April, can I have your cell?"

I handed him my phone. With a few taps and a smile, he added his phone number and his own ring tone. He handed the phone back to me.

"If you need anything, look under 'S' for Superhero and Superhero, Sr." Miles winked. "You never know when you might need to be rescued again. By the way, your ringer was off, I turned it back on for you."

"I still owe you that coffee, remember? Won't you please come in?" I begged, not wanting to be left alone with an angry aunt.

"Sorry, but I need to get the tour van back to the company parking lot. Coffee tomorrow?"

I glanced at Kate. "I'm gonna have to get back to you on that."

"Understood," said Miles, as he caught up with his dad.

Kate and I watched from the porch as the two handsome men closed the gate behind them.

"Again? What did he mean by again?" asked Kate.

A soft whimper came from somewhere near the gardenia bushes. Turning towards the sound, we spotted a pair of eyes looking at us from beneath the hedge. Lightning flashed, the drizzle changed to rain. A large, rust-colored dog crawled out from under the bushes, walked slowly over, and sat down in front of us.

"Is he yours?"

"No. I've never seen him before."

The rain fell harder.

"Can we bring him in? We can't just leave him out here in a storm. He's got tags on his collar. He must belong to someone."

Kate sighed, "Oh, all right. Bring him in. Leave him on the back porch. I don't want fleas in my house. I'll call his owner."

"He looks hungry. Is there anything we could feed him?"

"Roast beef in the fridge. Give him some water, too. Use the stainless, not the china."

I busied myself in the kitchen, happy to have the dog as a diversion. I wouldn't have to talk to Kate about my evening. At least not yet. I sat beside him while he inhaled his dinner. After he finished, I read his tag. *GUMBO* was engraved on the little dog bone tag. I ruffled his ears and whispered, "You're safe now."

"The number was no longer in service," said Kate as she came through the screen door.

"Can I keep him?" I asked.

"No! Tomorrow we'll take him to the address on the tag. Tonight, he sleeps on the porch. Here's an old blanket for him."

"If we can't find the owner, can we keep him?" I asked again.

"No, April. We need to find his owner and get the dog back home. And, tomorrow morning, you and I are going to talk about the ground rules for coexisting. I also want a full report on your evening: Miles, police, everything. Let's call it a night. It's been an exhausting day for both of us," said Kate, yawning.

"You have no idea," I muttered under my breath.

Kate locked the screen door and turned off the porch light. We headed to our respective rooms, closing windows along the way, but leaving the ceiling fans on for air.

Kate was right. I was very, very, very tired. It had been one long emotional roller coaster sort of day. I was totally on overwhelm and the storm wasn't helping matters. I was thankful to be inside, more than ready to call it a night.

I kicked off my sandals, pulled my tee shirt over my head, unzipped my skirt and let it fall down around my ankles.

Lightning flashed, thunder was immediate; the storm was nearly on top of us. The house groaned, the windows rattled against the wind; I knew I wouldn't sleep. I collected my clothes from the floor, balled them up and readied a pitch towards the chair. A small handmade Voodoo doll tumbled from the skirt pocket, landed at my feet and stared straight up at me. I froze.

Lightning lit the skies and thunder shook the house once more. *If this were some cheesy horror movie, the lights would go out about now. Cue creepy music.* A huge crack reverberated when lightning struck a tree in the front yard, severing a limb. The lights blinked out. A scream caught in my throat.

I dragged the tee shirt back over my head, felt around for my skirt, and bashed my shin on the dresser. The bedroom door creaked open.

"April, are you all right?" asked Kate. "I brought some candles and a flashlight for you."

"I'm fine, just fine."

I found the doll with my bare foot and nudged it under the chair. The doll was rough, scratchy against my skin; I shuddered at its touch. I took the candles and flashlight from Kate.

"Want some company?" asked Kate.

"No, I'm good."

"It'll pass quickly," she said.

"Good to know."

"Okay then. Try to get some rest. Good night."

"Kate?"

"Yes?"

"Never mind."

The bedroom door creaked closed.

"I'll oil that hinge in the morning," said Kate from the hallway. The house trembled again. "If you change your mind about company . . ."

The tiny doll was now an eight-hundred-pound gorilla in my room. *How did this stupid doll get into my pocket? Did the woman from the shop put it there? Why would she? What does she want from me? What does this mean? What should I do with it? Leave it under the chair? Put it in the trash? Throw it out the window? Ignore it? Return it to the store tomorrow? Would she accuse me of stealing it?*

This is every child's worst nightmare, a monster hiding under the bed. Or in my case, a Voodoo doll under the chair.

It was my nightmare now.

Because of the rain, I couldn't open the window. With no electricity, the ceiling fan didn't work. The room was suffocating; the burning candles sucked all of the oxygen out of the air. My skin was slick with sweat, my shin throbbed. Random thoughts paced like caged tigers in my head.

As suddenly as it started, the storm ended. The lights came back on. I snuffed the candles, threw open the window and stuck my head out. I filled my lungs with ion-charged air, replenishing the oxygen in my brain. I welcomed the last raindrops on my face.

I reached under the chair for the doll. It didn't look so frightening now. It was nothing more than small bits of fabric sewn together by hand with spooky, sightless button eyes. It was nothing I hadn't seen in that weird little shop. There were no pins sticking out of it, so that was good. I doubted there was reason for concern. It was the power people gave to the Voodoo dolls that was so frightening. Belief made the power real for them. Rational thought notwithstanding, I zipped the doll into my laptop case and stuck it in the back of the armoire. Now it was tomorrow's problem.

I listened to the sounds of the house. All was quiet. *Kate must be asleep.* I crept downstairs to check on Gumbo. The dog was pacing the sun porch. He looked like he could use a friend. That made two of us.

I led Gumbo into the kitchen, where I grabbed three of Kate's homemade cookies and a cold bottle of water. Upstairs, with Gumbo at my feet, I sat in the overstuffed chair and thought about my day. *Nothing makes sense anymore. Like Gumbo, I'm totally lost. Tomorrow, he'll be back with his family. And where will I be? I'll still be alone. No family except Kate, and clearly she's not thrilled to have me here. What would Dad say? What am I going to do?*

I climbed into bed and encouraged the dog to join me. Kate would be mad, but I didn't care. Gumbo was sleeping with me. Even with Gumbo beside me, sleep didn't come easily. Images of haunted houses, Voodoo dolls, and decaying cemeteries floated along the edges of my consciousness. Finally, just before dawn, sleep arrived. My first twenty-four hours in New Orleans had come to a conclusion at last. God only knew what the next twenty-four hours would bring.

Chapter Eight

I opened my eyes to intense sunlight and ungodly heat. The humidity was even worse here than Alabama. Gumbo, lying beside me like a large, furry heating pad, was snoring gently. *Oh, man, Kate's gonna be peeved when this dog comes downstairs with me!* The ceiling fan spun indolently, hardly moving the dense air. I sat up and ran my fingers through my damp curls and twisted them into a knot to get them off of my neck. I was hot and sticky, my mood as black as the Voodoo doll hidden in the armoire.

"Happy" rang out from my cell.

"What the heck?" I jumped out of bed, searched for my phone. The screen read *SUPERHERO*.

"Good mornin', Miss April! I hope you slept well, what with the storm and all," Miles said cheerfully.

"Fine, just fine, no problems at all. Slept like a baby," I lied. "Nice ringtone, by the way." I laughed and sat back down on the bed. "Do you call all of your girlfriends so early in the morning?"

"Naw, just you. Besides, it's eleven o'clock already. Where I come from, that's not early, that's brunch time. Will you join me?"

"Hmmm. Enticing, but I can't. We found a dog last night after you left. Kate wants to return him to his owner this morning. Can I buy you that coffee later today?"

"You most certainly may! Text me when you're on the way back. I'll swing by to pick you up."

"Deal. Later, Miles." I heard Kate outside my door.

"Are you up? I brought you some juice. There's a bowl of fruit and some yogurt and a muffin waiting for you downstairs whenever you're ready."

I opened the door a crack and took the juice from her.

"Thanks."

Kate sighed. "There's also some food and fresh water on the porch for Gumbo when you two come down. After you both finish, we'll take Gumbo home. Unless you have other plans?"

"Not 'til later. Coffee with Miles."

"He seems nice enough. You can tell me how you two met when we're in the car."

I didn't answer.

"Take your time, I'm in no real hurry this morning," said Kate as she turned to go. "Oh, and by the way, if that dog slept on the bed last night, put the sheets in the washer before you come down."

I closed the door, sat down and looked at Gumbo. He had soulful brown eyes and a happy tail, which thumped enthusiastically against the pillows. I didn't want to give him up. We were bonded now. I could tell. Gumbo jumped down and circled. He needed to go out. I finished the juice, zipped into yesterday's skirt and took him out to the front yard to pee. Stripping the bed would have to wait.

While Gumbo took care of business, I thought about the talk Kate wanted to have. Since I've never been big on sharing and didn't plan to start now, bonding with Kate wasn't high on my list of things to do. I needed a plan. I certainly wasn't going to tell her anything about the cemetery or the Voodoo stuff. I'd give Kate the abbreviated version of last evening while we searched for Gumbo's house. After the dog was returned to his family, I'd go have coffee with Miles and Kate would go to work. After that, I could go back to the Voodoo shop to return the doll. I'd finally be rid of it. Good plan. Simple enough.

I led Gumbo around to the back porch, where his breakfast was waiting. Inside, the kitchen was empty. Once again, the table was beautifully set. The food was tasty, the coffee was welcome. Kate sure knew how to treat her guests, both canine and human. While I cleared the table, Kate came into the kitchen carrying a slender brown leather belt, her handbag over her shoulder, keys in hand.

"I thought we could use this belt as a leash to get Gumbo into the car," said Kate. "What do you think?"

"It's a good color for him, it matches his eyes."

Kate rolled her emerald green eyes. "Ready to go?"

"I'd like to take a quick shower. Ten minutes?"

Kate eyed yesterday's clothes and said, "Take fifteen."

I slapped on a big smile. "Thanks for breakfast, Kate! Great muffin! You made it?" I asked, putting the last dish in the dishwasher.

"I did. Cinnamon apple with a caramel pecan crunch topping. It's a new recipe. You were my guinea pig this morning."

"Impressive," I said, now with an even bigger smile. "Just in case you changed your mind, I'll ask you again. May I please keep him?"

"No! Aside from the fact that he belongs to someone who is probably missing him, I don't want the responsibility that comes with owning an animal. It doesn't work for me." Kate continued, "And speaking of responsibility, let's get something straight. I'm your guardian now. No more stunts like last night. Going forward, your phone is to be on at all times. I need to know where you're going. I need to know who you're going with. I need to know what you're up to. This is non-negotiable. Go get ready."

My smile and I left the kitchen.

Thirty minutes later, I stepped out of the shower and tried to dry off. It was impossible. I felt like I needed another shower already. I dusted all of my nooks and crannies with the lavender-scented body powder that Kate left in the bathroom. It helped considerably. I braided my hair, slipped into loose clothing and sandals, and went downstairs to get Gumbo.

A few minutes later we were on our way. Kate had the top down on the Mini so I could take in the sights as we drove. The Royal Street antique stores and galleries were open for business. The sidewalks were crowded with multiple walking tours and the restaurants were busy with an early lunch crowd. The street hummed with activity. I didn't see a single building without people, plants, or wrought iron.

We came upon a cathedral and were stopped by a film crew angling for the perfect shot. I watched an actress dressed in a pastel hooped skirt and matching bonnet cross the church yard to reach a gray-uniformed Confederate soldier. They hugged, they kissed, she cried, he comforted. I heard someone call out "Cut!" and a young man wearing a headset directed us to move on. We inched our way through film trucks, tourists, and mule-drawn carriages until we were, officially, on our way. The car picked up speed, the breeze catching Gumbo's ears like sails in the wind. He seemed happy to be with us, which made me sad. It wouldn't be long before he was gone.

"Tell me about last night," said Kate.

"Not much to tell. I took your advice. I slept after you left. When I woke up, I was hot and hungry. I wanted to get out of the house, get some air, explore my new neighborhood, so I took a walk. I had dinner. I went on a tour of the city. A spur of the moment thing, you know? I assumed you'd think it was a good way for me to see New Orleans, get to know my way around. I wasn't wrong, was I?"

"You should have waited for me to show you around, to help you get acclimated. And, you don't ever need to go out to eat. There's always fresh food in the house."

"I didn't see any reason to wait for you. Can I finish now?"

"Go ahead."

"Miles drove the tour van and was our guide. When the tour was over, he asked to walk me home. I didn't think it was a good idea since I'd just met him. Good thinking, right? Anyway, the tour began and ended near the police station. After the tour, Miles took me inside to meet his dad. They both walked me home so I'd get back safely. That's it."

Kate stared out the windshield. She offered no comment.

I crossed my arms, sank deeper into the car seat. "I *didn't* do anything wrong."

Kate sighed. "Probably not. We'll cover ground rules for you later. I still need to figure out exactly what the ground rules are. Having a teenager in the house is uncharted territory for me."

I offered no comment, just stared out my window at the passing scenery. As the three of us cruised out of the city under a spectacularly blue sky, I caught myself relaxing for the first time in days.

Kate said, "The address on Gumbo's tag is located somewhere in the Ninth Ward. That's where the levees broke, remember? No, you probably don't, you'd have been too young. It's not so much a bad neighborhood, but a sad neighborhood. So many years since Hurricane Katrina and it's still not back to normal."

We passed astonishing road signs, *Gun-Free Neighborhood, Drug-Free Neighborhood.* We had definitely entered a different part of the city, one not frequented by tourists. People on their porches fanned away the heat, the insects, and the afternoon. The residents stared with curiosity as the cherry-red car with two white women and a dog rolled slowly through their bleak streets. They were suspicious of strangers, probably with good reason, although we hardly looked threatening. We made our way past empty, weed-covered concrete foundations and roadways that led to nowhere.

Dangerously unstable, abandoned homes stood as monuments to societal failure on so many levels.

"What does '2DB' mean?" I asked, as we drove by a barely standing house, with boarded-up windows, its front wall spray-painted with some sort of code.

"Two dead bodies," Kate replied quietly. "Homes were marked by search and rescue teams for collection of those who perished or needed to be rescued." Kate slowed the car and pointed. "See the four sections?"

I nodded.

"Each quadrant indicates something different, like which battalion was here, or how many people were inside, if they were alive or dead, or if they couldn't get in at all. See, over there? NE means No Entry."

There was no appropriate response for what I had just learned. I had never seen such abject poverty before. It was soul-crushing. I needed to get out of here. I looked for street numbers in earnest, trying to find Gumbo's home.

Once we turned the next corner, Gumbo began to squirm and whimper. We drew close to a yard where a tall, skinny African-American girl, somewhere north of thirteen years old, played alone. Gumbo began to bark, pulling at his makeshift leash. When Kate pulled to the curb, Gumbo launched himself over the side of the car, then knocked the girl down and greeted her with dog-slobber kisses. The girl squealed with laughter.

"Mama! Mama! Gumbo's back!"

I got out of the car. The girl stood up, brushed herself off, ran towards me and gave me the best hug ever. Gumbo jumped and barked, excited to be home.

"Angel! Honey, let go of that girl before you squeeze the life outta her!" An attractive, thirty-something, mocha-colored woman came down the steps, wiped her hands on her apron and approached the Mini. "Thank you for bringin' our Gumbo home. He's been missing about a week now, ever since he jumped out the truck when we were in the Quarter. Angel's been sorely upset." Gumbo glued himself to Angel, happy to be back with his human.

"Please, y'all come in for some sweet tea and cookies. They're fresh from the oven. We'd like to thank you proper," said the woman. "Angel, go fix up some tea, put some cookies on a plate for our guests. Napkins, too."

"That's not necessary, we're just happy it all worked out. We have to get back. Let's go, April," said Kate, motioning for me to come back to the car.

I watched Angel playing with Gumbo and felt really guilty for wanting to keep her dog. I threw a defiant look at Kate, turned back around and called to Angel, "I'll help you."

Chapter Nine

Kate got out of the car, pushed the damp hair from her face, and said, "It is mighty warm out here today. Tea would be nice."

"I'm Simone," said Angel's mother, extending a rough, never manicured hand. "You've a pretty daughter there."

"Thank you," said Kate, slightly uncomfortable. "She's April, I'm Kate."

"Let's all get to the shade," said Simone, following me up the uneven walkway.

The railing wobbled as I climbed the warped porch stairs. I almost lost my balance. Their home was beyond run-down, but the porch was tidy and looked scrubbed. Cushions on the weathered wicker chairs were worn, but clean; the potted plants flourished. Fresh laundry dried on a line in the side yard under the unrelenting afternoon sun, near a well-tended vegetable garden. Clearly they cared for their home, but didn't have the money for maintenance.

Angel held the ragged screen door open for Gumbo and me. Gumbo raced ahead, his nails clicking on the old wooden floorboards as he ran into the kitchen. The hallway was a personal gallery filled with dozens of old family photos. It was fascinating, a family history in black-and-white. It was like I had stepped into a time warp. There was no computer in sight. There was no hi-def TV. There was nothing that spoke of the twenty-first century.

"What are you doin'?" asked Angel.

"Looking at this picture."

"That one's my great, great, great, great maw-maw," she said, pointing to the small tintype of a woman with a turban wrapped around her head.

"Very nice. You look like her. Very pretty. You have her eyes . . . Let me take the tray, you bring the cookies, okay?"

After serving Kate and her mother, Angel and I sat on the porch steps. Gumbo lay down beside Angel.

"He's a good dog," I said, not knowing what else to say. Talking wasn't a problem, though, as questions flew from Angel.

"Where did y'all find him? Was he hungry? Did he miss me? Was he hurt? I was scared I'd never see him agin. Thank you, thank you, thank you," she said and threw her arms around me again.

"These cookies are quite good," said Kate, taking another bite and analyzing the flavors.

"My take on a old family recipe; I call them Angel Crunch Cookies. Lots of cinnamon, molasses, and pecans. My baby's favorite."

When the glasses were empty and the cookies were gone, Kate looked at her watch, set down her glass and rose to leave. "Oh my, I didn't realize it was so late. April, we should go now. I need to get ready for work."

"Will y'all come back sometime to see me and Gumbo?" asked Angel, walking with me to the car, Gumbo at our heels.

Kate opened the car door. "It was nice to meet you and your mother and Gumbo. I'm glad it worked out. April, let's go!"

Angel's face fell.

"I'll try to come back, I promise," I said.

An impish grin split Angel's face. "You have to come back. I wanna ride in that car!" I watched Angel run back to the house, laughing, Gumbo loping behind her.

Kate pulled away from the curb, made a U-turn, and we were on our way. I got out my cell and texted Miles: *On our way back. Coffee?*

"Well, that was different," said Kate.

"Nice people . . . I feel sorta bad for not wanting to return their dog."

"I can imagine. Clearly she loves her dog . . . By the way, April, I overheard you talking to Angel about their old family photos. There are two boxes of our family photographs stored in the attic. I intended to scan everything into digital albums but never got around to actually doing it. Is this something you can do for me? The photos might help familiarize you with some of your own family history. You know, fill in some of the blank spaces? It would be a great help to me." Kate hesitated. "What do you think?"

"Paid position?"

"Free room and board not enough for you?" laughed Kate.

"Can I get a dog?"

"No!" said Kate, not laughing now.

We pulled up in front of Kate's house. Miles was already waiting on the porch, lazily rocking back and forth in one of her white wicker rockers.

Kate greeted Miles warmly. "Thanks for taking care of April last night. You two go have a nice time."

Kate turned to me. "You and I will talk later."

We made our way up Royal to St. Ann Street, headed towards Café du Monde.

Miles slipped into his tour guide patter. "Café du Monde opened in the French Market in 1862. It's open twenty-four/seven, except for Christmas Day and sometimes during hurricane season. Even though their property suffered only minor damage during Katrina, the owners closed for several months to renovate the dining areas and the kitchen. The café is famous for two things: French-style beignets, sort of like a donut only better, and their special café au lait, a slightly bitter coffee drink, half hot milk, half coffee with chicory. The only other menu items are fresh-squeezed orange juice, iced coffee, and milk, either white or chocolate."

"What's chicory?"

"It's the root of the endive plant. During the Civil War it was roasted and blended with coffee to stretch their meager supplies."

"You're a walking Wikipedia!"

We approached the shaded, bustling patio. "Before we grab a table, let's go around to the back of the building. I want you to see the kitchen at work."

An enormous picture window was fitted into the back wall of the kitchen. A large man, wielding an oversized rolling pin, hands and arms covered in flour, flattened a massive piece of pastry dough on an old butcher-block counter. When the ancient wooden checkerboard-style cutter scored the smooth dough into small squares, the next batch of beignets was ready to fry. The cook stepped close to the fryer, turned around, and began to expertly flip the dough squares over his shoulder into the vat of bubbling oil.

"Look at this place! Look how fast everyone moves! Oh my gosh! I've never seen such a huge deep fryer! That oil looks pretty black—it's not lard, is it?"

"Nah, it's just plain ol' Louisiana cottonseed oil."

"Look how the dough puffs up when it hits the oil," I said, pointing to the little pastry pillows.

"After they hit the oil, they get flipped over once by the guy with the long-handled strainer, then they're ready to go."

After they were drained and plated, the beignets were covered with a generous amount of powdered sugar and handed to waitresses, who practically ran them out to the customers.

"Shall we go in, partake of the fine fare this establishment has to offer?" asked Miles, using his silky tour guide voice.

"Well, yeah!"

When our order was delivered, I dove in. The first bite blanketed me with powdered sugar. Miles laughed and wiped my chin.

"Oh my God, that's good!" I said, finishing the first one.

I wiped my fingers and looked at Miles. "Your dad seems pretty cool. Where's your mom? Any brothers or sisters?"

"Hold on there. Slow down, little lady," said Miles. "It's just me, my dad, and our bloodhound, Nosey. Mom lives in Georgia with my stepdad; no brothers, no sisters. I don't see them very often. I used to spend every school holiday and every summer with her, but now not so much. I don't have the time, I work nights full-time during the summer. Most days I volunteer for construction work, rebuilding homes for people in need. Believe it or not, there's still a lot of work to be done in the Ninth Ward."

"I absolutely believe it. I was just there this morning to return the dog I told you about. This poor little girl and her mother, they need so much help! It was heartbreaking! I don't get it."

"Well, until things change, it's up to the rest of us to do what we can to help . . . So, tell me, what's the scoop on you? Are you staying at your aunt's house for the summer? Are your folks on vacation or something? Do you have any brothers or sisters?"

"No brothers, no sisters." I hesitated. "My plans are a little up in the air. Can we talk about something else?"

"Ah, a woman of mystery!" Miles changed the subject. "Listen, would you like to spend tomorrow with me? I'm going out to work on one of the houses. You can tag along, if you like. Maybe you can help with food or something? Your aunt is probably busy anyway. I keep tee shirts in my car for volunteers, I'll give you one to wear. What say you, my fair lady? Are you game?"

My mouth full, I mumbled, "Sure."

Washing down the last of the beignet with café au lait, I said, "*Laissez les bons temps rouler.* I heard that in a movie once."

"Let the good times roll! You're sounding like a native already!" Miles checked his watch. "Would you like to take a carriage ride around the French Quarter?" he asked after paying our bill. "I promise to keep the running commentary to a maximum."

"Will it take long? I told Kate I'd do something for her," I fibbed, knowing what I really wanted to do was get rid of that creepy Voodoo doll.

"Maybe an hour or so, does that work for you?"

"That works."

Mule-drawn carriages were lined up in front of Jackson Square, waiting for their next passengers. We walked across the street to the first one and while Miles paid the driver, I petted the mule's soft muzzle. The carriage squeaked and groaned under our weight as we climbed in and settled onto the worn red leather seats.

"Would you like to hear about Jackson Square? Or Jax Brewery?"

"No, I'd like to hear more about you."

"Well, I just finished my first year in the Architecture program at Tulane. The rebuilding projects through their community outreach program is a win-win situation for me. I learn something new almost daily and I stay in shape from the physical labor." When Miles flexed an impressive bicep, my heart skipped a beat.

"I get to give back to a community that desperately needs it and I get loads of practical experience in eco-friendly home building, which is my passion."

"Why did you stay after Hurricane Katrina? So many people left and never came back."

"My dad stayed. Mom and I moved to Georgia while New Orleans tried to pull itself together. The chaos here was unimaginable. Dad's sense of responsibility kicked into overdrive. He wanted to stay to help maintain some semblance of law and order."

"Wasn't it really dangerous?"

"Well, yeah. That's why they needed dedicated police officers like my dad. I'm not sure New Orleans will ever fully recover. But the good news is our community is working its way back and we're proud of our efforts!"

"That's great," I murmured. I hesitated briefly before continuing, "Uh, Miles?"

"Yes?"

"What do you know about Voodoo?"

Chapter Ten

Miles, taken aback by the dramatic shift in subject matter, became wary. "Why do you ask?"

"No reason, just curious. That shop we visited was kind of interesting."

"I gave you most of what I know on last night's tour. I know it isn't something you want to be involved with."

"Why not? Is Voodoo like witchcraft or something?"

"Personally, I think most of it is a lot of hype. Though from what I've heard, parts of it can be pretty gruesome. There have been rumors of ritualistic killing of animals as offerings to the gods or spirits or priestesses, whatever they're called. It's rarely talked about, and then only in whispers in certain neighborhoods. Black magic, spells, chanting—it's all a little too 'out there' for me. Like a cult or something."

"The shop you took us to didn't look all that dangerous. It seemed like a place for tourists to do a little out of the norm souvenir shopping for their friends back home."

"Looks can be deceiving. You saw only what they wanted you to see, the commercial side. Nobody knows what goes on behind closed doors after business hours."

"Hmmm. Okay," I said, remembering the locked door behind the African weaving.

I needed to give more thought to what Miles had said, but not now. All I wanted now was to lean back and enjoy the sights and

Miles for the rest of the carriage ride. I could decide what to do with that stupid Voodoo doll later.

"You must not have gotten enough sleep last night," said Miles.

I opened my eyes, looked up at Miles and realized that we were already back at Jackson Square, me with my head resting comfortably on his broad shoulder, him gazing down at me.

"Why do you say that?"

"Well, you snoozed for almost the entire carriage ride. Either you needed the rest or I was totally boring and I seriously doubt that. By the way, did you know you have the cutest little snore?"

My cheeks flushed all the way to my curls. "I don't snore!"

Smiling, Miles helped me down from the carriage. "Touched a nerve, did I?" He tipped the driver and turned back to me, "Mademoiselle, it is time for me to return you safely to your home. I need to get ready for work."

"Not to worry, I can find my own way back. Thanks though." I turned to go.

Miles took my arm and rolled his eyes. "I don't doubt that for a minute, but my car is still at your house. We might as well walk together."

We walked through the French Quarter in shy silence. No matter where I looked, there was something interesting to see. Miles, sensing I wasn't up to it, held off on further historical commentary. I could easily understand why this city was such a mecca for tourists. But a home for me? I simply couldn't wrap my head around it. Didn't want to. As we got closer to Kate's place, I had to laugh when I spied a real estate sign that advertised *APARTMENT FOR RENT*, with a smaller sign hanging beneath that said *NOT HAUNTED*.

At the front gate, Miles bowed and kissed my hand. "Until tomorrow."

Slightly embarrassed, but thoroughly enchanted, I said, "I had a nice time today." I watched Miles drive away and whispered, "Thank you."

Inside, I found a note from Kate hanging on the refrigerator door:

There's cold roasted chicken, Cajun potato salad, and sweet tea for dinner. Fresh lemon cookies are in the jar in the pantry. I'll be home between 9 and 10. K. P.S. The boxes of photos are on the floor next to my desk if you want to get started. Thanks. K.

That's nervy! I never actually agreed to help with her family photos. It's nice that she fixed dinner for me, though. I looked at my watch; it wasn't even six o'clock yet. There was plenty of time to get the doll back to the Voodoo shop. But how would I explain to the shopkeeper why I was returning a Voodoo doll that I never paid for in the first place? Maybe she wouldn't be working and I could just hand it over to whoever was manning the shop. That would be good, really good. That shopkeeper kind of creeped me out. I wouldn't mind not seeing her again. I should go now, get it over with. Should I have something to eat first? *No!* I was stalling, I needed to just go! I climbed the stairs with leaden feet. I didn't really want to go back to the Voodoo shop, but was too curious about the doll not to go.

I took the little black figure from its hiding place in the laptop case. I inspected it closely. Its rough black fabric and tiny button eyes held no sign of evil in the daylight. It wasn't really something to be afraid of, right? I couldn't tell what it was stuffed with, but it smelled faintly of sage and felt like straw. *Isn't sage what people burn to clear out evil spirits? Is this why I have it? To remove evil from my life? Are there evil spirits in my life? Does that woman sense something ominous in me, around me?* I had to stop this. I was totally over-analyzing and freaking myself out. It was just an *accident*. The Voodoo doll fell into my pocket when I slammed into the shelving. Nothing more, nothing less. I needed to get over it already, get the darned thing out of here. I stuffed the doll into my bag, raced out of the house, and, hopefully, headed in the right direction to get to the shop.

After a few wrong turns, I approached the Voodoo shop with trepidation, unsure if I was doing the right thing by coming back. I should have just thrown the darned thing out. *What is the matter with me? Where is my head?* I slowed my pace, slowed my breathing. I needed rest. I needed to find peace. My mind buzzed like a busy beehive; too much sugar, too much caffeine, too much grief, too much change, too much unknown. My life was moving faster than I could process—"Warp Speed, Mr. Sulu," said Captain Kirk in the recesses of my mind. *What am I afraid of? The doll? The shopkeeper? Myself? Life? The future? Breathe in, breathe out. Breathe in, breathe out. IT'S ONLY A STUPID DOLL! It's only my life.*

As if it had a mind of its own, my hand reached for the doorknob. The door creaked open.

"Welcome, Miss April," said the shopkeeper with the pale gold eyes. "You are right on time."

Chapter Eleven

"On time? For what? How do you know my name?" I asked, now thoroughly discomfited.

"Nothing mysterious. The shop is about to close. Your timing is good. You told that nice young man your name last night. You have nothing to fear from me."

"I'm *not* afraid!" I reached into my bag for the doll. "I'm only here to return this to you. It must have fallen into my pocket when I knocked all of the dolls off the shelf." I shoved it at her, turned to go.

"Miss April, wait! I placed the doll in your pocket."

I whipped around to face her. "How dare you! What for? Why me?"

"I sensed your pain. If you returned with the doll, I would have an opportunity to speak with you alone. I believe I can help you."

"I'm fine! I don't need any help! Especially your kind of help! Voodoo, hoodoo, what kind of fool do you think I am?"

"Not foolish, just hurting. My dear, you are angry. Very, very angry. Anger can eat you alive." She moved closer to me. Her golden eyes looked deep into mine. "After you left last evening, Miss April, I put some things together for you. For when you returned."

I stiffened. "Things? What things? How did you know I'd come back?"

"Please take this," she said, reaching for a bag by the counter.

"Why give me anything? You don't even know me," I snarled, impatient, angry with myself for still being there.

The shopkeeper said nothing, just studied me with her peculiar gold eyes. It was nearly impossible to tear myself away from her gaze. Totally creeped out, I was ready to bolt. My mind said no, but my hand said yes. I took the heavy bag from her and backed slowly towards the exit.

"I'm not paying for this!" Running out the door, down the steps, still clutching the bag, I reached the sidewalk and looked back. The shopkeeper was gone, the lights were off, the shop now closed. The alligator head above the door laughed at me, sending shivers down my spine. The sky was filled with dark, puffy clouds; the smell of rain was in the air and the wind had kicked it up a notch. Like the night before, the street was empty. It was déjà vu all over again. I felt like some twisted Alice in Wonderland, who'd fallen into a black magic rabbit hole. My head said, *Drop the bag! Leave it behind!* But my hand wouldn't listen. I raced through the French Quarter and after a few more wrong turns, arrived breathless at Kate's house, my hand white-knuckled from gripping the bag. I unlocked the front door, climbed the stairs to my room, and dropped the Voodoo goodie bag on the bed. I paced the room, all the while staring at the bag.

Cripes! What am I supposed to do with this stuff? Why did I take the bag from her? Why did I bring it home with me? Wasn't the whole point of going to the shop in the first place to get rid of that stupid Voodoo doll? I must be out of my freakin' mind!

It was too big to hide in the laptop case; I wrapped a blanket around the bag and stuffed everything into the armoire. I hoped it would be enough to keep the bag away from Kate's prying eyes if she snooped around in my things, as I had with hers.

I went into the bathroom and threw cold water on my face. I'd need to shower again before bed. *Doesn't the heat and humidity ever let up? God, I hate this place.* I was sweating like a pig. *Do pigs sweat?* I had no idea. Drained and fighting a sugar headache, I went down to the kitchen for something cold to drink.

Kate's note was still on the refrigerator. I'd completely forgotten about the food she fixed. I was starving. Having had only cookies and beignets since breakfast, I now craved protein and salt. Opening the fridge, I was unsurprised to see it well stocked and organized. At least I would eat well if I had to live here. I loaded up a plate, grabbed a bottle of chilled water, and carried a tray out to the glass-topped wicker table on the front porch. I turned on the carriage lights and the ceiling fans, settled myself on one of the rockers, and watched the tourists hurry past. Bright, jagged lightning split the sky in the distance, thunder rumbled soon after, the trees swayed as the wind picked up; another storm was rolling in. *Perfect, just perfect.*

Numb from my day, I began to eat. The food was fabulous, but I had a hard time appreciating it. I was exhausted beyond comprehension. Resting my head on the back of the rocker, I watched the ceiling fan spin lazily overhead. *What would Dad do if he were here? First, he would hug me. Next, he would scold me. Last, we would hit the Net to learn what we could about Voodoo. We would approach the situation logically. That was how we always did things. Together. Now I'll have to do everything alone. However, I don't need to do anything right away.* My energy was completely sapped, and resting here for a few minutes seemed like a good plan to me. I closed my eyes and crashed.

Chapter Twelve

I awoke with a start when a boisterous group of people passed in front of Kate's house. All were carrying oversized plastic cups from a frozen daiquiri shop in the French Quarter. None appeared to be bothered by the impending storm.

I didn't understand the attraction to the fluorescent colored slushy rum drinks, but alcohol wasn't my thing. The few drinks I'd tried at a party back home in Alabama were overly sweet and made me sick. The kids at school thought I was an uppity outsider. Of course I wasn't. *Outsider, definitely, but uppity? Me? Not a chance.* Aside from being underage, I prefer being in control. If my attitude put me outside the "in" crowd, so be it. I didn't care. Dad worked as a consultant upgrading I.T. systems for different companies, moving from city to city to city. We were never in one place for very long. Making friends wasn't really my thing either. *Who cares what anybody thinks anyway?*

I finished the last bits of food, picked up my tray, and went inside. I put the dishes in the dishwasher and the tray back on the sideboard and got another bottle of water. It was impossible to stay hydrated in this heat. I picked a lemon cookie from the clear glass jar in the pantry and took a bite. It was tart, not overly sweet. I helped myself to three more and headed upstairs. *So much for no more sugar.*

Instead of going directly to my room, I detoured at Kate's office. Like everything else in the house, her office was well organized, yet it was cozy and informal. Lace curtains hung on either side of the French doors that led to the balcony. Bookcases with glass doors filled one wall from floor to ceiling; a varied collection of cookbooks occupied the bottom half, leather bound classics and legal tomes were higher up. It was a nice-sized room with a small closet and a door that led to the bathroom. The furniture was antique (big shock), but the computer and the printer/scanner/fax were brand new. I crossed the room, opened the French doors and listened to the laughter and music floating in on the gardenia-scented breeze.

The old leather banker's chair squeaked when I sat at the desk. I opened the center drawer. Pens, Post-its, paper clips, and 3 × 5 note cards were housed in a wire mesh drawer organizer. The large desk drawer on the right contained Kate's household files. The drawer on the left held hard-copy recipe files. I tapped the keyboard, the screen came up. *No password protection, not a good idea.* I double-clicked on an intriguing icon. *Well, this is interesting. Kate is writing her own cookbook. One of her secrets?* She hadn't mentioned it to me. Then again, we hadn't talked all that much since I arrived. And, so far our conversations had been a little less than friendly. According to the file date, this was her latest draft. I clicked through her recipes until I found the lemon cookies: almost no sugar, loads of lemon juice and zest, with plain Greek-style yogurt. The cookies were soft, chewy, creative, and yummy. Leaning back in the squeaky leather chair, I rubbed my eyes. Tiredness was taking over. My mind wandered to an unhappy place.

I never got to know my mother very well; her fault, not mine. What I did know, I didn't like. Growing up, I always felt the Army totally suited Mom's personality. She was cold, unfeeling. And, of course, absent for most of my life. I never understood what my dad saw in her. Still can't. It must have been the sex. Although I had difficulty imagining that she ever gave herself fully to him. All I knew was she never gave anything of herself to me the few times she graced us with her presence over the years. What a waste her visits were. Why did she even bother? Some sick sense of maternal responsibility? Well, she slammed that door shut seventeen years ago.

And, how about Kate? She appears to be my mother's polar opposite. She definitely isn't all buttoned up and self-absorbed like her older sister. But, it's clear Kate still has unresolved family resentments. One could say we have that in common.

I closed my mind to the bitter memories, then closed the cookbook folder and browsed the other icons. Kate had already set up a folder for the soon-to-be-scanned family photos.

On the floor next to the desk were two small, dusty old cardboard boxes of photographs. Unlike everything else in this house, the boxes were not organized. Everything had been thrown in and, judging from the amount of dust, never looked at again. I had expected it to be a quick and easy gig, but that wasn't the case. I'd have to organize everything myself before I began scanning. If I started working with the photographs now, I could put off looking at the bag of Voodoo stuff until later. Kate would be home soon. Going through the bag was something better handled when I wouldn't be interrupted, maybe later tonight after Kate was asleep.

I moved from the chair to the floor with my water and cookies, started sorting through the pictures: color in one pile, black-and-white in another. I would separate the two piles chronologically later, as best I could, anyway. Some of the photographs were so old, they pre-dated Polaroid. The resolution wasn't good on any of them. I wondered if Kate had Photoshop? I got up, checked the computer's program list. No Photoshop. *Note to self: ask Kate to buy Photoshop.* I should be able to clean up a lot of them.

From the quick color/black-and-white sorting, I could tell that almost all of them had been taken before my mother's hasty departure from New Orleans seventeen years earlier. Unless there was another box in the attic, it appeared that very few family photos were taken after she left. Maybe the family broke then and couldn't be put back together. How sad for them. How sad for me. I had been denied in a way I could neither understand nor explain. This was going to be a lot harder than just organizing photographs. This was like trying to piece Humpty Dumpty back together again to make a "family portrait." One that I'd had no part of until yesterday.

I sipped my water and finished my cookies while I deliberated how to proceed. Start with the oldest black-and-white? Or, would the color photos go faster? I began to turn over the black-and-white photos. There was little or no information on any of them. I'd just have to go with my best guess as to the sequencing, using clothes and cars as my guide. Maybe Kate could help with identifying the "who and where" after I took care of the "when." I started with the ones that looked the oldest—no gloss, just photos that looked like they had been rolled onto the paper. They had a kind of silvery sheen and were slightly faded. They hadn't been very well cared for. I soon got into a rhythm and became immersed in the project.

This, this is my family! I'd never given any thought to Mom's side of the family before. She never talked about them and I never bothered to ask. I didn't care. Mom was more like an out-of-town guest whenever she visited during her infrequent furloughs. She certainly didn't act like my parent, or my idea of what a parent should be. And now, I'll never have the opportunity to ask my dad about her. Even though she dumped him and left me on his doorstep, my dad loved her until the day he died. Go figure. At some point in their complicated relationship, they must have gotten wise to birth control, because I have no siblings. *Totally fine by me.*

I put the brakes on that train of thought and started sorting through more photographs. I came across a few old photos of

African Americans, probably dating back to the early to mid-1800s. *Who were they? House servants or plantation workers or, God forbid, slaves? It would be odd, though, keeping photographs of the servants, right? Whoa! What the . . . ?* Stunned by the next picture, I stopped sorting.

The photo of a woman with a turban wrapped around her head was almost identical to the picture I saw hanging in the hallway of Angel's house. According to Angel, the woman was her great, great, great, great grandmother. *Was it possible this same person worked for my ancestors? That's feasible, right?* I had no way of knowing anything about her, but maybe Kate knew.

My legs were cramped, I needed to get up and move around. Collecting the empty water bottle, the plate, and my phone, I headed back down to the kitchen. Before leaving the office, I slipped the photo of the woman with the turban into my pocket. I'd ask Kate about it when she got home tonight. My cell rang; it was her.

"Hey, what's up?" asked Kate. "Everything okay? Just thought I'd check in."

"All good."

"I wanted to let you know that I'm going for drinks after work and won't be home until later. Will you be okay on your own?"

"Why wouldn't I be okay?" I asked sharply.

"Is my going out a problem for you?"

I took a deep breath and huffed, "No."

"You sound like it's a problem. I thought you'd be happy to have some time alone."

"It's not a problem. Really. Go ahead, go . . . Word of advice, though. If you've got a date, you need something a little sexier than that chef's jacket and clogs you've got on. I hope you have something in your locker."

"Oh, I think I can manage." Kate laughed and disconnected the call.

Thunder shook the house—the storm was getting closer. The trees in the yard twisted against the rising wind, their shadows danced across the living room walls. The floorboards creaked overhead. *Is there somebody else in the house?* I jumped when the French doors slammed shut upstairs. *Why does everything in this city feel so bloody haunted? Maybe it's just me. Maybe I'm the haunted one.* I shivered even though it wasn't cold. *What is up with all the shivering? Am I getting sick?* I turned on the stove light, a lamp in the living room, and the chandelier in the dining room. Before returning to Kate's office I scanned each room for boogeymen. Finding none, I climbed the stairs, stopped halfway up, and went back to turn on the porch lights for good measure.

Back to the photos? Or go through the Voodoo goodie bag? I looked at the clock; I had plenty of time.

Bag it is.

Chapter Thirteen

Outside, the wind was howling, tree branches scratching at the windows. Inside, the curtains flapped as if trying to escape the windy assault. The house squeaked and groaned under the weight of the powerful wind. *Did I lock the front door? The back door? Did I even unlock the back door when I came home? I don't remember.* I was reasonably sure I closed all of the windows downstairs and had locked all of the doors. Lights were on, everything was locked up tight; all was secure. That didn't stop me from wishing I had Gumbo, or a dog like him, to keep me company. I hoped the thunderstorm would pass us by; I couldn't bear to close my window again.

I stared at the armoire. *I can do this, I know I can. There's nothing to be afraid of.* I threw open the doors, yanked out the bag, and dumped the contents onto the bed. There were books, black candles, incense cones with a burner and a tiny brown bottle of oil. There was also a beautiful red and black gauzy scarf. Underneath it all was another Voodoo doll and a gris-gris bag. I dropped the scarf back over the doll and the gris-gris bag and backed away. *Make a decision!* I began reloading the bag to take back to that woman, but stopped when I saw a letter addressed to me lying on the floor. I picked up the cream-colored envelope and stumbled over to the comfy chair. *This is, officially, beyond bizarre.*

Should I open it? How could I not open it? I'd never know what the letter said if I didn't open it. I turned the envelope over. A glob of red wax with a fleur-de-lis sealed the flap. Nice touch. It looked like Kate's butter pats, only blood red instead of pale yellow. Good stationery—scented, too. I sniffed. *Gardenia?* I got up, retrieved a letter opener from Kate's office, and slit the top of the envelope, careful not to break the pretty seal. The cream-colored card was embossed with a small gold fleur-de-lis.

> *Ma chère April,*
>
> *You are reading this, so good for you, you have taken the first step in overcoming your fear of the unknown. You will find in your bag: "The New Orleans Voodoo Handbook" to give you some history, "The Voodoo Hoodoo Spellbook" to give you understanding, and "Women and New Orleans: A History" to give you inspiration. I hope you enjoy the books.*
>
> *I invite you to visit me when you are ready to delve deeper and learn how to use the rest of the items.*
>
> *À bientôt, Marguerite*

I reread her handwritten note before sliding it back into the envelope. *Is she serious? Delve deeper? What does she mean by that? Do I even want to know?* I had to admit, I was sort of intrigued by her. She was refined and elegant, and appeared to be well-educated. But there was something unsettling about her. She was a little spooky, otherworldly. I couldn't quite put my finger on it, but there was definitely something different about her. She was being nice and trying to help me. But why? She put together this Voodoo swag bag for me. Again, why? What was her motivation?

I went back to the bed to inspect the items. I stacked the books and put them in the armoire, so Kate wouldn't see them. It couldn't hurt to flip through them at some point, could it? After all, they were only books. I placed the candles on the dresser. If Kate ever asked about them, I'd tell her I bought them in case the lights went out again, black being my favorite color. I picked up the tiny brown bottle labeled *Holy Anointing Oil* and read: *For spiritual strength, dab forehead and temples.* I opened the bottle, took a whiff. I didn't recognize the fragrance, but it wasn't unpleasant. As directed, I dabbed a little on my forehead and temples, inhaled deeply. Not so bad—not bad at all. I slipped the bottle into my handbag.

I picked up the fringed red and black scarf and wrapped the gauzy fabric around my shoulders. It was large, more like a shawl. I put the incense cone on the burner, found last night's matches, and lit the peak. I danced around the room, twirling with the shawl. I was beginning to feel other-worldly myself. I flopped back down in the chair and laughed long and loud, getting into the *spirit* of things. Or maybe I was finally just losing it.

The wind died down; the air was hot and still. The house, at last, was silent. Since it hadn't rained, it was even more humid. Ugh! The cloying smell of incense hung in my room like an odorous fog. I'd better try to air out the room before Kate came home. I glanced at the clock; she would be home soon. I removed the shawl, wrapped the Voodoo doll and gris-gris bag inside, and placed everything in the armoire. I was ready to call it a night when "Happy" sang out from my phone. It was Miles.

"I thought you were working."

"I am, but I have a few minutes before everyone gets back on the van. We're still on for tomorrow, right?"

"Tomorrow?"

"You said you wanted to go with me to the housing project. Volunteer your time, talent, and good humor, remember?"

I'd forgotten.

"Of course I remember! What time?"

"Nine o'clock?"

"I'll be ready and waiting."

"Okay, then. Sleep tight, don't let the bedbugs bite."

"It's so hot in here, I doubt they have the energy."

I heard someone downstairs. "Gotta go, Miles, Kate just got home."

"And, you'd rather go see her than talk to me? Ouch!"

"See you in the morning!" I laughed, ending the call.

I found Kate in the kitchen, unloading her tote bag. She looked amazing in a turquoise off-the-shoulder top, a black pencil skirt, and four inch peep-toe stilettos.

"You keep that outfit in your locker?"

"I do," she smiled sheepishly. Kate tossed her chef's jacket and pants into the laundry basket, put her clogs by the door.

"Where did you go?"

"We went to the Napoleon House."

"Napoleon House, like *the* Napoleon?"

"Yes. Napoleon intended to live in that house. Believe it or not, his supporters planned to spring him from exile and bring him here to rule as King of New Orleans. The plan was a bust, but the name stuck. If you'd like, I'll take you there to eat. They have great gumbo."

"What else?"

"They have panini, too."

"Not food! Your date. Tell me about it!"

"Well, let's see. He's a flipper."

"A flipper?"

"He buys houses, renovates them and sells them at a profit, then he starts the process all over again."

"Anything else?"

"I told him about you, well, as much as I know anyway. He said you sounded *spunky* and would like to meet you when you're up to it."

"*Spunky?*"

"His word, not mine. I'd have to go with *snarky*."

I ignored Kate's own bit of snark.

"Relationship material? Not that you need a relationship or anything."

"Who said anything about wanting a relationship? He's just a friend. We had a drink, that's all."

I got up to get some cold water. "I started looking at the family photos today. Before I can organize anything, I need to ask you some questions, get some background, for the tags for the jpegs. F-Y-I, I left piles of pictures scattered everywhere in your office. Are you open to buying Photoshop? I might be able to clean up the pictures somewhat after I scan them."

"Thanks for the heads up. I won't go into the office until you get more organized. Let me think about Photoshop, although it would probably be good to have it."

"Okay, great! Oh, and Kate?"

"Yes?"

"I'm going with Miles tomorrow to help at the housing project where he volunteers. Are you okay with that?"

"You should have asked me first. I'll let it go this time, because I think it'll be good for you. You need to make friends here. Do you know if you'll be there all day?"

"Dunno."

"Well, when you do, let me know, okay? It's late, you should get some rest. I need to get out of these heels," said Kate. She started for the stairs.

"Kate?"

"Yes?"

"Nothing."

I followed her up the stairs. We said our good nights in the hallway and closed our doors.

No longer ready to call it a night, I settled into my comfy chair, booted up my laptop and got to work. I typed in *Voodoo* and came up with 13,200,000 results. Even Wikipedia had a gazillion different categories to choose from. I needed to narrow my search parameters. *Where should I begin?* Scrolling down through the first page of choices, I came across "Louisiana Voodoo." I opened the link and found that it, too, had subcategories, but not as many.

Okay, let's see what we have here. Basically, it's a religion with West African roots brought to America by slaves; it is distinguished from other practices by the use of gris-gris bags and Voodoo dolls. I totally get that!

What exactly is a gris-gris bag? I typed in *gris-gris bag* and found over sixty-five thousand results; one of the first links led to a book in my swag bag. Holy cow! Instructions for making a gris-gris bag! All I'd need was some red cloth or leather, herbs, charms, and maybe some bones. *Bones? What kind of bones? Where would I get bones and, hang on a minute, why am I even thinking about how to make one anyway? Okay, this is getting a little too weird.*

On overload, I closed the browser, shut down the computer, and got into a steaming hot shower to relax the knots in my neck. I generously sprinkled the lavender powder over my damp skin, slipped into an oversized tee shirt, and climbed into bed. My phone vibrated from an incoming text: *looking forward to tomorrow. M.*

I turned out the light and, with a smile on my face, fell into a deep and, thankfully, dreamless sleep.

Chapter Fourteen

Startled awake by the phone's alarm, I was groggy and grumpy and my tee shirt was wringing wet. I was nearing the end of my clean clothes and needed to do laundry, especially the sheets, which still smelled like Gumbo. I checked my phone for e-mails. Along with the usual junk mail, there was one from Sam letting me know it would take longer to settle my dad's estate than he originally thought. He asked if I needed anything. *How touching.* I wanted to send him a howler screaming, *"Yes, I need something! I need my life to go back to normal!"* But normal was never going to happen. I opted for polite: *Please send money and the rest of my clothes. Thanks for checking. A.*

I needed to get ready or I'd be late for Miles. I raced through my morning routine, which now included a generous sprinkling of lavender-scented dusting powder, and headed to the kitchen. Kate wasn't there, but she'd left another note on the fridge:

Needed to run out, help yourself to whatever you want for breakfast. Wasn't sure what you & Miles had planned for lunch. I packed some food and a thermos of iced coffee for you, just in case. Have fun. K.

Armed with juice and a muffin, I went outside to have breakfast. Kate was working at making me feel welcome, even though my arrival in her life was an unwelcome surprise. I was grateful to have some time alone this morning. *Alone.* That's what I was now.

Raising my eyes to the sky, I wanted to scream, *"How could you do this to me, Dad? Leave me like this? You were my rock. You were always there for me. What am I supposed to do now? Get on with my life? How's that supposed to work? YOU never had a 'what if' plan in case of emergency. YOU had to go and have not only an emergency, but a FATAL emergency. It's no longer 'what if' but 'what now?'"*

I refused to cry, I was too pissed. I sat in the courtyard, agitated to the max. When the doorbell punctured my unhappy reverie, I realized I'd been wallowing in self-pity for so long, I'd lost track of time. Miles was here.

I ducked into the powder room for a quick once over in the mirror. I didn't look nearly as damaged as I felt. I plastered on a happy face and got ready for the day ahead.

"Mornin'!" said Miles.

"Good morning. Would you like to come in? Have you had breakfast? I could fix you something to eat if you're hungry."

Miles stepped into the hallway, "Nah, I had breakfast already, but thanks for asking."

He looked around, admiring the architecture. "Nice place."

"Kate fixed some lunch for us. She's a chef, you know. Should I bring it?"

"A chef, really?"

"She is."

"Then, yes, absolutely bring it! I made some peanut butter and jelly sandwiches for us, but I doubt they would even hold a candle to what your aunt fixed!"

"Peanut butter and jelly? You are such a little kid!"

"Part of my charm, don't you think?"

Now my smile was real. "Yep, definitely part of your charm."

Miles handed me a lime green tee shirt with a Tulane logo on the front and *VOLUNTEER* plastered across the front and back. "We should hit the road."

I shrugged the tee over my tank and pointed down the hallway. "Would you please grab the insulated bag and thermos off the kitchen counter? I'll go get my purse."

I raced up the stairs, reached for my purse, and, in my haste, knocked it over instead, spilling the contents everywhere. Hurrying to collect everything, I found the little bottle of anointing oil. I read the bottle again: *For spiritual strength, dab forehead and temples.* What could it hurt? I dabbed my forehead and temples, inhaled deeply and put the bottle on top of the dresser.

At the top of the stairs, I stopped and took a moment to appreciate how unbelievably handsome Miles was and to wonder what he saw in me.

He turned, looked up at me, and asked, "You okay?"

"Never better."

"Nice perfume," he said, opening the Jeep's door for me.

"Ummm, thanks."

Miles guided the Jeep slowly through the French Quarter to avoid spooking the mule-drawn carriages filled with tourists.

Miles began again, "Jackson Square was named after . . ."

"Please! Enough already with the tour guide routine! I'm on information overload," I faux-complained, putting my hands over my ears.

"You mean I can impress you no further with my vast knowledge of our beloved history? I am wounded to the core," said Miles, doing his best Rhett Butler.

"Okay, then, tell me about yourself," he said.

"Why?"

"Why not?"

"My dad and I moved around a lot."

"Why?"

"Because we just did. That's why."

"You must have loads of friends all over the place. Anyone special?"

"No, no friends. Nobody special. Too many schools. No interest in getting involved."

"Okay, then, what does your dad do?"

"Miles, can we talk about something else? Maybe you can give me another history lesson?"

"Okay, my mysterious maiden, we'll do it your way. How about I throw out some random facts that you could use at parties or when a conversation lags?"

I nodded. "Sure, why not?"

"Did you know that New Orleans was the first Confederate city to be captured by the Union and was occupied the longest by the Yankees during the Civil War?"

"I did not know that."

"Did you know that in 1791, the first two West African slave ships to arrive in the United States landed at the Port of New Orleans?"

"I did not know that either. Should I be taking notes?" I asked.

"Okay, here's a really creepy one for your next Halloween party or Girl Scout campfire. Did you know that the small crypts that fill some of the walls in New Orleans's oldest cemeteries worked like ovens because of the heat and the humidity? That the vault interior heat accelerated the decomposition of bodies and created a process of slow cremation?"

Aghast, I stared at Miles. "Seriously? A weirdly disturbing factoid like that would certainly be an ice-breaker! I must say, this is quite the educational first date we're having."

"Date?" said Miles lightly. "Let's just call this hanging out together. If by the end of today, you're still interested, we'll talk about a real first date . . . You will still be interested, won't you?"

"I'll think about it."

"Of course, take all the time you need, as long as the answer is *yes*."

"Yes!" I laughed. "Tell me about the work you volunteered me for today."

"There are a number of humanitarian organizations that worked, and are still working, to restore the Ninth Ward. Habitat for Humanity and Make It Right are just two of them. Harry Connick Jr. and Branford Marsalis worked with Habitat for Humanity to build a new village and beautiful park for the displaced musicians of New Orleans. We're going to drive right by it."

"Marsalis. He's a musician, right?"

"Yes, he is, so is his father and his three brothers. Brad Pitt—you may have heard of him—established the Make It Right Foundation in 2007. His commitment not only helped the community, but the environment as well. Everything has been built as 'green' as humanly possible. There's a lot of innovative stuff happening here. For an aspiring—and might I add, handsome—architect, I've had the opportunity to work with cutting edge design and construction techniques. It's been a phenomenal experience for me."

"That's great! How nice for you that you can pursue something you enjoy and obviously have a talent for." I waited a beat, then eased into the next subject, "Miles, is there anything more you can tell me about Voodoo? I'm really curious about it and was thinking I might want to go to a real Voodoo ceremony."

"You want to do what? Go to a Voodoo ceremony? *Why?*" asked Miles, bewildered. "It's not something you can just go to, like a concert or something. You have to be invited by someone in the inner circle, a devotee. Clearly, I'm *not* that guy."

Miles's face clouded as we drove through the impoverished neighborhood in an uncomfortable silence. I chewed on my bottom lip while I processed what to say next.

"Um, I'm sorry, Miles. I promise I won't ever ask you again about Voodoo . . . Is this the part where I should drop in one of those random factoids you gave me because our conversation is lagging?" I tried to make light of the situation.

Miles shook his head and sighed. "You are a handful, Miss April, no doubt about it."

He slowed the Jeep in front of the construction site. I was surprised to see we were just down the block from Angel's house, angered to see that parked at the curb in front of Angel's house was Kate's cherry-red Mini Cooper.

What's she doing here? Obviously, she doesn't trust me. She's spying on me.

I opened the Jeep door and jumped out, ready for a fight.

Chapter Fifteen

Before another angry thought could cross my mind, Angel, with Gumbo at her heels, ran towards me.

"You came! You came!" Angel skidded to a halt in front of me. "Your Auntie's already here," she said, leading me down the cracked, uneven sidewalk. Angel looked back at Miles. "Well, don't just stand there!"

Miles pointed to the construction site, started to speak, but changed his mind and caught up with us. Gumbo galloped ahead and beat us up the porch stairs. Kate, surprised to see us, rose too quickly, splashing her skirt with tea.

"What are you doing here?" Kate and I asked simultaneously.

"I left my belt here yesterday. I brought this for Gumbo," replied Kate, dangling a new leash in front of me.

I narrowed my eyes. "You mean you're not here to check up on me?"

"What? You can't be serious. How on earth would I even know you'd be here? You never told me where you two were going, remember?"

Angel tapped Miles on the arm, whispered, "Are they always like this?"

"Don't know," said Miles, leaning against the railing to watch the show.

A loud crack caught everyone's attention. We watched in horror as Miles was propelled backwards into the yard, arms and legs whirling like helicopter blades, scattering broken railing pieces far and wide over the dirt. Miles landed with a horrendous thump.

"My Lord!" shouted Angel's mother. "You all right?"

Gumbo howled at the commotion as we scrambled from the porch to help Miles. He rose gingerly, avoiding a plethora of rusty nails.

"Take my hand. It's my turn to rescue you," I said, helping Miles to his feet. "Are you hurt?"

"When was the last time you had a tetanus shot?" asked Kate, eyeing the debris.

"I'm good. Not hurt. Recent tetanus shot. Mandatory for construction work." Miles dusted himself off.

I circled him, looking for wounds. *Nice butt*, I thought.

Angel held Gumbo by his collar to keep him out of the rubble. Kate tossed her the leash. "Use this," she said.

"Let's clear this stuff out, load up the Jeep and take it down to the dumpster before someone gets hurt," said Miles, leaving the yard.

When Miles returned with the Jeep, he pulled work gloves from his pocket and handed a pair to me. "Sorry I broke your railing, ma'am. I can fix it for you," he said, collecting the broken pieces.

"No matter, so much is broken. Just look around," said Simone.

I helped Miles clear away the rotted wood. After loading the last of the porch railing into the Jeep, Miles tied a red rag around several pieces.

"What's that for?" asked Angel.

"So nobody gets too close," said Miles.

"Are you gonna fix up our house?" asked Angel.

"I'll try," said Miles.

Angel squirmed a bit, then blurted out, "Can you get a bike for me?"

Miles hesitated, "You want a new bike?"

"It doesn't have to be new, because it'll be new for me," laughed Angel.

Miles grinned, crossed his arms, and asked, "Anything else?"

"A dress for my mama, a steak for Gumbo . . . and a job for my mama, that'd be good."

Miles laughed. "Do you think I'm some kind of fairy godfather or something?"

"Maybe," she giggled.

"What are you two up to?" I asked, approaching the Jeep, followed by Kate and Gumbo.

"Nothin'," said Angel.

"Nothin'," said Miles, winking at Angel.

"I've got to go get ready for work. You're staying to work with Miles, right?" asked Kate.

I looked at Miles, "Okay with you?"

"Heck, yeah! The morning's been so interesting, I can't wait to see what the afternoon brings!" Miles laughed and petted Gumbo, while I said goodbye to Angel.

"Thanks for comin' back to see me. Come again soon?" asked Angel.

"I'll try." I gave Gumbo another ear snuggle and got in the Jeep with Miles.

"Are you sure you're okay? That was a spectacular fall, totally YouTube-worthy!"

"Nah, it was more classic, like an old episode of SNL with Chevy Chase. You know what I'm talking about, right?"

"I do."

Miles backed the Jeep up the street and into the construction site driveway, stopping in front of the dumpster to unload.

"Can you rebuild their porch railing soon? Those steps were pretty rickety. Can you do those at the same time? We don't want Angel or her mother to get hurt, do we?" I asked.

"I'll check with the crew to see if we have any spare lumber. It shouldn't take much. My dad and I could probably knock out a new railing and new steps over a weekend. With your help and Kate's food, of course."

"Can you get Angel's mom added to a list or something? Maybe you can get their whole house redone, or maybe a new home altogether?" I asked, rolling with the idea. "There's got to be something we can do to help!"

Miles turned his head and looked over his shoulder.

"What are you doing?"

"I'm checking to see if there's a sign on my back that says SUPERHERO or FAIRY GODFATHER!"

"Who said anything about a superhero? But, now that you mention it, you would look pretty amazing in tights!"

"Amazing? Me? You sweet talker, you!"

At the site, the workers were on lunch break.

"Miles, can we eat before we get started? I'm starving!"

Miles grabbed the insulated bag, I got the thermos, and we joined the others. After brief introductions, Miles and I found a spot in the shade and unpacked the bag, which, in addition to lunch, included a cold pack for the food and hand sanitizer wipes; Kate thought of everything. She had prepared another incredible meal—roasted chicken sandwiches on olive bread and a side of red-bean-and-rice salad for each of us. She also sent three dozen assorted cookies for the crew.

Impressed, Miles said, "Your aunt is beyond awesome. How long will you be staying with her?"

"Like I said the other day, my plans are a bit up in the air."

"Well, however long you stay, you're going to eat well, that's for sure," said Miles, finishing the last of his repast. "The guys will be way happy to see homemade cookies! Since we don't have much of a snack budget, our food supplies are always a bit slim. Your aunt is going to spoil us." Miles looked at his watch. "We have a little time, are you up to a guided tour?"

"Bring it on!"

Miles led me out of the shade and off the site. We walked up the remains of what used to be a sidewalk. We made our way farther up the block, moving away from the most desolate part of the neighborhood where Angel lived and closer to a brand-new housing development.

"These houses up here are part of the Make It Right project. Brad Pitt brought in twenty architects to design eco-friendly housing to replace the homes lost to Katrina. They have more than half of the hundred and fifty homes completed so far."

I was impressed by the lovely new homes. They all had different designs, there was nothing cookie-cutter or rudimentary or cheap-looking about any of them. Most were built above ground, some with enough room underneath to park cars.

"Look up there," said Miles, pointing to a roof. "See that square? That's an escape hatch. Most people in the Ninth Ward kept an ax in the attic, so they could chop their way out in case of a flood. Now, if it happens again, all they need to do is open the hatch, climb out and wait to be rescued."

"What? It can't happen again, can it? The government repaired the levees, didn't they?"

"I know they've spent billions rebuilding and upgrading to guard against another failure. Only time and the kindness of Mother Nature will tell."

"Why are there still so many uninhabitable homes?" I asked, eyeing the other side of the block, seeing nothing but weeds and more dilapidated structures.

"I think a lot of people couldn't afford to rebuild. Either they didn't have any insurance, or enough insurance, or they didn't qualify for government assistance because they couldn't provide proof of ownership. Whatever the reason for abandonment, I can't begin to imagine how hard it was for them."

My resolve was absolute. "Let's get to work. Show me where to start."

Even as hot as it was, my energy was unfailing. The afternoon passed quickly. I got tools, I stacked lumber, I brought water to the guys; wherever I could help, I did. At break, I brought out the cookies and iced coffee. Miles was right about Kate's homemade cookies—they were a huge hit with the guys and were perfect with the iced coffee. Miles might be right about Kate. I wouldn't say she's beyond awesome like he says, but she does know her way around a kitchen. That didn't mean I wanted her as my guardian, though.

I didn't need a guardian. I could take care of myself.

Chapter Sixteen

"You look done in," said Miles as the Jeep rolled to a stop in front of Kate's house.

"How observant of you," I said wiping the sweat from my face with a tissue. My shirt was filthy, I could only read *VOLUN* because dirt covered the balance of the word *TEER*. My arms and legs were streaked with more dirt and my hair was a fright wig after driving in the ragtop Jeep.

"I'm surprised you let me back in your car the way I look!"

"You look amazing," said Miles, blushing.

I waited a beat. "I had a nice time with you today. You took me out of myself. Thank you. It felt good to do something worthwhile."

"Maybe we can do this again sometime? Maybe a real date next time?" Miles asked.

"Maybe we could," I replied, slowly getting out of the Jeep.

Miles honked, gave a backward wave, and pulled away from the curb.

I limped up the porch stairs, not sure which would be best, a hot bath to ease my aching muscles or a cold shower to relieve the heat. Maybe both. Definitely something cold to drink and some sort of anti-inflammatory were in order.

There was another note from Kate on the fridge.

I made a pitcher of fresh lemonade with mint for you. There's plenty of food. Help yourself. I won't be home for dinner, but I won't be late. Hope you had a nice day! K.

I wondered what her game was. *Is she honestly nice? Or is she just being overly polite? Trying to make up for all the lost years, make up for her disinterest in me? Whatever. It doesn't matter to me either way.*

I took my lemonade upstairs, undressed, and removed my watch and earrings. I placed them on the dresser next to the photo of the woman in the turban, which I'd forgotten to ask Kate about. *Note to self: ask her tonight when she gets home.* It's probably nothing mysterious, just the cook or the housekeeper, somebody like that. I stood under the cold, stinging shower and let my mind drift. Miles was something special: smart, handsome, kind, funny, and talented. Did I mention handsome? And, those muscles—what could a girl say about his biceps except *WOW!*

I toweled off and reached for the container of lavender body powder. With the unrelenting heat and humidity, Kate must have to buy this stuff in bulk. I wondered briefly if I should thank her for leaving it for me, but decided against it. I wasn't ready for any sort of bonding.

Famished, I headed to the kitchen, bringing two of the Voodoo books with me for a little light reading during dinner. I refilled my glass with lemonade and loaded a plate with last night's roast chicken and potato salad. I sat at the kitchen table and dug in. Flipping through the first book, I stopped mid-chew. Taken aback by a portrait, I dropped my fork, ran to get the photograph out of my room. Racing back to the kitchen, my heart was pounding.

I compared the two pictures side by side. *It's her! What on earth? Why is this picture of Angel's great, great, great, great grandmother in our house? Who put this picture with our family photographs? Does Angel know that her great granny was a Voodoo queen? Does Kate know anything? What is she hiding from me?*

No longer hungry, I threw my meal in the trash. Hoping to find some answers, I scanned the chapter titled "The Voodoo

Queen: Marie Laveau" in *The New Orleans Voodoo Handbook*. My brain processed only bits and pieces of information as I skimmed the pages:

Born in 1801. Grew up in the Treme suburb. First husband, Jacques Paris disappeared. Died? Returned to Haiti? Nobody knew. The two children she bore by Paris died from yellow fever. She called herself "Widow Paris." She worked as a hairdresser. She captured the heart of an aristocrat, a white Frenchman named Christophe Glapion. She bore him between seven and fifteen mulatto children. Nobody could verify how many.

Summer, 1859, the local newspaper, The Crescent, *referred to her as "the notorious hag who reigns over the ignorant and superstitious as the Queen of Voodoos." A neighbor complained about "the hellish observance of mysterious rites of Voodou."*

The wind picked up again, branches raked the house, thunder rumbled in the distance; another storm was on the way. The house, dark except for the overhead light, began to creak and moan again. What was with all this creaking and moaning? This house, the hot, humid, unpredictable weather, everything was getting on my nerves. *I am so over New Orleans!* Restless, I got up, refilled my glass with lemonade, sat back down at the table, and continued to read, still only processing bits and pieces:

Officiating at public dances at Congo Square . . . Laveau's home was filled with candles, statues and images of various saints. St. John's Eve (June 23) ceremonies at Lake Pontchartrain. Once semisecret gatherings . . .

Lightning flashed, thunder shook the house. I screamed when something touched my shoulder.

"I guess you didn't hear me come in."

"Shit! Don't ever sneak up on me again! You scared the crap out of me!" I shrugged her hand away.

"Watch your mouth!"

I stood and shoved the photograph in front of her face. "Who is this?"

Kate paled. "What are you doing with that?"

"You asked me to help you with the pictures, remember? Family history, good for me and all that. Remember? Who *is* this?" I demanded.

Kate pulled a chair away from the table and sat. "Sit down and be quiet! We need to talk."

"No! I'm not sitting."

"Get something straight, April. You live in *my* house, you don't get to demand anything. You've made it perfectly clear you don't want to be here. Fine. Guess what? None of this is easy for me, either. I *never* wanted to have children. Now I'm stuck. Stuck with you!"

I dragged a chair across the hardwood floor, as far away from Kate as I could get. I sat, crossed my arms tightly against my chest and glared at her.

"You are so much like your mother, feisty, full of fire. And, you *absolutely* inherited her ability to piss people off."

Kate picked up the Voodoo books. She narrowed her eyes and stared directly into mine. "Where did you get these?"

"Not relevant." I waved the photograph at her once more. "Tell me about her! Put an end to the secrets and the lies. Lay the *family skeletons* to rest!"

Kate sat vibrating with anger.

"Who is this woman?" I roared.

"She is your great, great, great, great grandmother."

Chapter Seventeen

"What?"

Kate didn't answer.

"This woman is *family*?" I threw the photograph at her. "You didn't think that was something I should know? Are you kidding me?"

Kate's steely gaze chilled me; her voice was low, controlled. "What was I supposed to say when you arrived, April? Welcome to New Orleans! I'm your aunt Kate and oh, by the way, your great, great, great grandmother was a high priestess of Voodoo, a free woman of color? Seriously?"

"My life just keeps getting better and better. Every day is such a joy for me." I paced, unable to be still. I stopped in front of the ancient kitchen mirror. My skin was a startling shade of white in the glare from the overhead kitchen lights.

"Why do you have to be the one to tell me? Why didn't my own mother talk to me about any of this? I wouldn't have cared! She's my mother! I'm her daughter! I'm supposed to be family. I should have been told!"

"And what a family we are! Self-righteous parents, a runaway sister, and a bratty niece . . . For what it's worth, I planned to talk to you about everything eventually. You needed to get acclimated first. You needed time to grieve for your father. You needed time to adjust to a life with me. God knows, I needed to adjust to having *you* in my life. Still do . . . Honestly, I'm surprised this photo was packed away with the others. Our parents did their level best to bury Mother's heritage."

"If they kept everything so well hidden, how did you find out?" I asked, pacing faster now.

"Ironically, the same way you did. I found this photograph and wanted to know who she was. My mother, who was more than one mint julep over the line, told me in a moment of unapologetic candor. She was neither proud, nor ashamed, just matter-of-fact. The shame, well, that was all on our father. He was a dyed-in-the wool racist. I doubt he would have married her if he had known. He lived by the one-drop rule."

"What's that?"

"It was a law which stated that if a person had one drop of black blood in their family, they were considered legally black."

"Why don't I look black? Or you, your skin is as fair as mine. We couldn't be more white. I don't understand any of this."

"It's simple genetics. Dominant characteristics of race can disappear after only three or four generations. Look it up on the Internet if you don't believe me. Read up on Thomas Jefferson and his slave Sally Hemings. Marie Laveau had as many as fifteen mixed-race children. Even if she had only half as many, that's still a lot of opportunity for interracial relationships over the years."

"What about the Voodoo? Is that inherited, too? Is that why the lady in the shop . . . ?"

"What lady in what shop?" asked Kate.

"Nothing, never mind. Forget I said anything."

"What lady? Answer me!"

"Everything about my life just sucks! I hate New Orleans! I hate living with you! I'm done." I headed for the door.

"You know what? I don't much care for you. Or your bad attitude. I don't want to live with you either," Kate shot back.

I stomped out of the kitchen, watching as Kate picked up one of the Voodoo books and threw it across the room. When it hit the wall, her grandmother's beautiful antique mirror fell to the floor, shattering into a million pieces.

I grabbed my purse from the hall table and flew out of the house. The wind was almost gale force, the rain came down in sheets. Streets were empty, no carriages or cabs were in sight. *Perfect, just perfect,* I thought, slogging my way up the sidewalk fighting against the high winds and heavy rain.

I didn't have a plan. I didn't know where I was going. I didn't know how far I'd gone until I arrived at the Voodoo shop. The storm raged all around me. Soaked to the skin and in need of shelter, I turned the knob. The door was locked. A razor thin stream of light shined at the back of the shop; somebody had to be inside. I rapped on the door, but nobody answered. Finding an unlocked gate next to the building, I went through and followed a muddy path to the back porch. I stopped before knocking. *Is this what I really want to do?* When the back door swung open, the decision was made.

"Welcome, Miss April. Come in out of the storm before you catch your death."

Chapter Eighteen

The wind gusted, blowing stinging rain into the back porch. I scuttled through the doorway like a drowning rat in search of a dry hole. I couldn't get any wetter, but I could get dry. The woman disappeared into a small room and returned with a stack of fluffy towels.

"Dry yourself. I will find you something to wear."

I rubbed my face and toweled my hair, worked my way down my arms and legs, kicked off my sandals, and dried my feet.

"Here, put this on," she said, handing me a long multicolored dress.

"Is there somewhere I can change?"

"In there," she said, pointing to the bathroom door. "I will go fix some tea for us."

Closing the door behind me, I looked in the tiny mirror, thought about the crash I heard after I left Kate's kitchen, and wondered briefly if she was okay.

I am a mess, no doubt about it. My life is in shambles. I have no friends except maybe Miles, if I haven't scared him off. I have no family except Kate, if I haven't scared her off. Seems to me that at this point in my life, the only ally I have is this Voodoo woman. What does that say about me?

There was a rap at the door.

"Are you all right, Miss April?"

"Coming," I said, slipping the soft, flowing fabric over my head. I opened the door.

"Let's have some tea; you can tell me what brought you to my doorstep this night. But first, wrap your hair, it will dry faster," she said, handing me a thin, brightly colored towel.

Gathering my curls into a knot, I wrapped the turban tightly and was freaked out by my reflection. I looked exactly like a white Marie Laveau. Queasy and lightheaded, I glanced in the mirror again. I didn't look anything like her, it was only this outfit and my overactive imagination. I removed the head wrap, left it on the counter, and followed the woman. Sliding the woven fabric aside, the shopkeeper guided me through the door. The dimly lit room was filled floor to ceiling with all things Voodoo: statues, draped fabrics, and hand-crafted dolls were scattered everywhere. Candles shimmered in crystal votive holders, the stale scent of long-extinguished incense lingered in the air. If there was a window anywhere, it was hidden. Large cushions for devotees surrounded an altar littered with offerings, like the ones I'd seen at Marie Laveau's crypt. A china teapot and two delicate cups had been placed on a table near the altar. The woman motioned for me to sit down.

"I have tea cakes if you are hungry."

"No thank you," I said, settling onto a soft, oversized cushion.

Pouring the tea she said, "I hope you like chamomile."

"I do."

"I added a few herbs of my own. I hope you find it pleasant," she said, handing me the steaming cup.

"Do you own this place?"

"Yes. I own the building; I live upstairs and have the shop down here."

"What is this room?" I asked, taking in my surroundings.

"This room is used for private events. Please tell me what brings you to me this stormy night, Miss April."

"I don't know. I just came."

"For what purpose?"

"I have questions."

Marguerite studied me and smiled. "I had a daughter about your age, very much like you. Oh, did she have a mind of her own! So smart, so inquisitive. She very much wanted to go to college, to study cultural anthropology as I had done. She wanted to go to Africa, to do good works."

She paused, lost in her past. "She was taken from me, in a car crash, my husband, too. Life can be so fleeting, so devastating."

I nodded my head in understanding.

"But you know that already, for you have suffered a great loss, *n'est-ce pas?*"

I nodded again.

"You have questions, my child?"

"I looked you up on the Internet. You're not an ordinary shopkeeper. You're a Voodoo high priestess, aren't you?"

She tilted her head, but did not answer.

"Can you tell me if after someone dies, it's possible to contact them? Is that what Voodoo does? Like a séance or something?"

Marguerite searched my face before replying. "Is that what you want, to contact someone who has died?"

"Maybe. I'm not sure. I was just thinking that . . . Yes, I do. I need to contact someone."

"In Voodoo, we can make contact with spirits, the *Loa*, through ritual."

"What kind of ritual?

"There are many, but for you, a spiritual cleansing or healing ritual would be necessary to unblock your energy if you have had a catastrophic life event. Perhaps a death in your family? When your positive energy is released, it will be possible to have a psychic connection with the one who has passed."

I didn't know what to say, so I said nothing.

Marguerite continued, "Miss April, there is something we can do now if you like. Would you be open to a Tarot reading? I can perform a three-card interpretation for you—one card each for your past, present, and future."

I hesitated, then nodded yes.

"Shall I begin?" she asked.

Again I hesitated, but nodded yes.

Marguerite rose to get her Tarot cards. She handed the deck to me and said, "Shuffle until you feel the energy is right."

Not sure what energy I was supposed to feel, I shuffled several times and handed the cards back to her. The building shuddered as the storm's violence intensified; the lights winked out. In the shadows of the flickering candles, Marguerite appeared more sinister than sincere. Totally creeped out, but fixated all the same, I held my breath while the high priestess split the cards into three separate piles.

Turning the top card from the first stack face up, she tapped it once with a well-manicured finger. In a deep, somber voice she said, "*DEATH*. This card represents your past."

The Death card! Oh my God! This can't be good.

"For you, my child, *DEATH* signifies an uninvited change in your life, your fear of the unknown . . . Shall I go on?" she asked.

Unable to speak, I nodded a yes.

Turning the top card from the second stack over, she tapped it with her polished nail and said, "*NINE OF SWORDS*. This card represents your present. It is the card of anxiety and sorrow. You despair, yet you seek comfort and spiritual healing."

I was stunned. The first two cards were disturbingly accurate about everything happening in my life.

"Last one?" she asked.

"Yes," I squeaked. I needed to know what the future card held for me. Marguerite took the top card from the third stack and turned it face up. She tapped one last time.

"*JUDGMENT.* This last card suggests you will soon make reckless decisions. A trial by fire awaits, to unshackle you from your fears. In the end, you shall be freed."

"What does that mean, *trial by fire*? I don't understand."

"My dear child, it is a metaphor. You have faced and will continue to face challenges. You will continue to be tested. Ultimately, you will be released and restored."

My mind raced to process what Marguerite had said. My voice trembled when I asked the high priestess, "Do I need to be . . . do I need to be *spiritually cleansed*?"

"That is for you to decide, my child."

Chapter Nineteen

Confused, scared, unable to make any decision, I composed myself as best I could and changed the subject.

"I, uh, I have another question for you. In the bag of Voodoo things you gave me, there was a note from you that said if I wanted to delve deeper, I should come to you. What did you mean?"

"Miss April, when you came to my shop that evening, I felt an energy from you, a connection of sorts. Have you dabbled in Voodoo before?"

"No! The only thing I ever knew about Voodoo came from hokey old movies I watched with my dad on popcorn nights . . . My great, great, great, great grandmother did, though. She more than dabbled. She was a queen."

Marguerite fell silent. "Who was your maw-maw? There is only one real queen, you know."

I gazed deep into her pale gold eyes. "Marie Laveau."

She smiled. "Ah, yes. Marie Laveau was not *a* Voodoo queen, she was *the* Voodoo Queen. She set the standard for all who have followed. There has been no other like her."

Marguerite stood, removed a book from a shelf by the door, and thumbed through the pages until she found what she was searching for. She looked at me, looked at a page, then back at me. She pointed at the picture. "You see, there is a resemblance, it's in the eyes. You have her eyes. I now understand the energy I felt from you. It is why you fainted that night in the shop. You were connecting psychically with her *Loa*. My shop is not just a tourist attraction or *trap*, as some call it. This is a place of worship and spiritual guidance for true believers."

"Whoa. Let's get one thing straight. *I am not a believer!*"

"You say you do not believe and yet, you are here. Fate has directed you to me, Miss April."

Overwhelmed by tiredness, I lay back on the pillows and closed my eyes.

"Me? Directed? No. I have no direction. I'm lost, alone. I have been ever since . . . since my dad died . . . I never got to say goodbye to him."

"My child, it is time for you to say goodbye. You and I, we shall raise his spirit together. We shall connect with his *Loa*. We shall cleanse you, unblock you. After which, both of you shall be at peace."

"Peace. That's good. I need peace," I mumbled. I was feeling odd, not quite with it any longer. "You know what else, Madame? I have new cousins. They're black, like me," I whispered.

My head was spinning. No, it was the room that was spinning. *What's happening to me? I can't think straight. What was in that tea? Did she drug me?* Sweat dripped from every pore, soaked my dress. Utterly unaware of my surroundings, I was in a deep, dark place, a place from which I might never return. In the recesses of my mind I heard voices, angry voices coming from far, far away. I didn't want them to wake me, I wanted to sleep, to be left alone. *Everyone go away! Leave me in peace!*

A large, warm hand gently shook me. "April, wake up. It's me, Miles."

"Miles? You smell nice. What time is it? What are you doing here? Where am I?"

"Why, Miss April, I am here to rescue you once more. How many times is that now? Too many to count! This time I brought the big guns with me."

I sat up, peeked around Miles. *Uh-oh.* I looked down at my dress, scanned the room, and remembered where I was.

"Did she hurt you? Did she give you drugs?" asked Detective Baptiste, very much in protective detective mode now.

"What? Who? Marguerite? No, she didn't drug me. She took me in out of the storm, gave me dry clothes and some hot tea. Chamomile. I fell asleep. End of story."

I shook my head, tried to break the cobwebs loose. I tried to stand up, but was wobbly and fell back against the pillows. Miles offered both hands in support. Grateful for the assist, I held them both, finally got up.

"This is definitely not the end of the story, young lady! Disappearing into the night in the middle of a tropical storm? Not bothering to call? Since I couldn't reach you, I assume the ringer was off on your phone again, after I specifically told you to keep it turned on. And how on earth did you end up asleep in this Voodoo shop? This is so not the end of this, young lady. I'm responsible for you, remember? You are so grounded. Grounded for life. Or, at least for the length of your life with me!" railed Kate.

Wide awake now, I stiffened, wrapped my arms tightly around myself and said, "Fine. Whatever. I won't be here much longer anyway. Remember, trust fund at eighteen? I can do whatever I want."

"Oh, no," retorted Kate. "That money is for college. If you don't use it for school, the funds revert to me. I told you, your grandfather was very controlling and not a nice person."

Detective Baptiste whispered to Miles, "Are they always like this?"

"Seems so," he replied.

"Okay, everyone, let's wrap it up here, get April back home," said Detective Baptiste. He turned to Marguerite, "Madame, I advise you to stay away from April."

Marguerite handed me my neatly folded, still damp clothes and turned to face the detective. "Officer, you have no cause for concern. I mean her no harm. Miss April is a . . . troubled young lady, *n'est-ce pas*? Who am I to turn her away if she seeks my counsel?"

"Look, lady, I don't know what game you're working here, but you'd better stay away from my niece! I'm warning you!" said Kate, thrusting a fist in Marguerite's direction.

Marguerite turned her pale gold eyes on Kate. "Was that a threat, Auntie? Officer, you heard that. You are my witness." She waved her hand dismissively, "Leave, all of you! Miss April needs her rest."

"Thank you for helping me, Marguerite. You have been very kind," I said.

Kate dragged me out of the shop and pushed me towards the detective's unmarked car. She bundled me into the back seat and slid in beside me. In front, Miles buckled up, his dad turned off the police car's flashing lights and pulled away from the curb.

Trying to break the tension, Detective Baptiste asked, "Beignets, anyone?"

"Perhaps another time," growled Kate.

Miles glanced in the rearview mirror, watched me lean against the window, as far away from Kate as I could get. I knew he had questions, but they would have to wait. A few minutes later, the police car rolled to a stop behind Miles's Jeep. Miles and Detective Baptiste got out and offered to get Kate and me safely inside.

"No thank you. I've got it from here." She shook Detective Baptiste's hand and gave Miles a big hug. "Thank you, both. Sorry to drag you out in the storm tonight, to make you a part of this."

I looked at Miles and his father, "Sorry for causing so much trouble for you both."

"All's well that ends well. But you really need to stay away from that woman," said Detective Baptiste.

"Yes, sir. I'll do that."

"April, let's go in. We've all had enough for one night."

I turned back, gave Miles a little finger wave and a brief smile, and mouthed *Text me*. He winked and gave me a half smile before taking off in his Jeep.

Kate and I trudged up to our respective rooms, both completely spent from the evening. When I spread out my damp clothes to dry, I found that Marguerite had secreted another scented note. I broke the wax seal, opened the envelope and read the invitation and directions to a spiritual cleansing ceremony the following evening.

> *Please come and bring your cousin. I shall meet you both at the*
> *dock at 7PM. From there, I will take us to the ceremony.*
> *À bientôt, Marguerite*

I was stunned. *My cousin? I guess she means Angel? Oh my God! I have a cousin and an aunt, or would Simone be a cousin, too? Wow, just a few days ago, I had no family. How many more of us are there?*

I couldn't handle any more tonight. I'd think about all this stuff tomorrow. I slipped out of my dress and into my bed and slept the sleep of the dead.

Chapter Twenty

The aroma of something divine baking in the kitchen wafted up the stairs. Nothing would be divine once I came downstairs for breakfast. Kate was extremely irritated with me—in her mind, rightfully so, but I disagreed. On the one hand, she did come to my rescue last night. But, on the other hand, she didn't trust me or I wouldn't be grounded for life. I picked up Marguerite's dress, folded it, and tucked it away in the armoire with the rest of the Voodoo gifts, thinking I should get it dry cleaned before returning it.

In order to avoid going downstairs as long as possible, I took my time deciding what to wear for the day, tidied my bedroom, and had a long, cool shower. With nothing left to do, I crept down the staircase. An explosion of baked goods filled the kitchen. Muffins, cookies, cakes, and fresh bread covered almost every available inch of counter and table space.

"Having a party?"

"I bake when I'm angry," she snapped.

"You must be pretty angry," I said, a nervous little laugh escaping.

"Ya think?" Kate whipped around to face me. "You know, April, my life was just fine until a few days ago when you blew into it like a tornado. I had order. I had structure. I had peace and quiet. I don't have any of that now. You've disrupted my entire life. Honestly, I'm not sure I want your chaos in my life. So, here's the deal, *you* are going to take today and figure out how *you* can make this work for us."

Shaken by the vitriol, I quietly took a seat at the table.

"You need to find a job. The newspaper is on the counter by the toaster. I already circled some potential opportunities, all of which are walking distance from here. It's time you take responsibility for your own life and your own actions. I'll be here to help you along the way, as long as you cooperate. I could be a good friend if you let me. You need to give one hundred percent to make this work, otherwise, when you turn eighteen, you're on your own. Understood?"

I didn't answer right away. I studied Kate; her clothes were covered with a light dusting of flour, her hair was uncombed, dark circles under her eyes gave them a sunken appearance. She looked exhausted and exasperated.

"I'll give it some thought and get back to you."

"Really? You're going to get back to me?" roared Kate.

Since I didn't have any place else to live, it was probably in my best interest to not piss her off any further. "That didn't come out right. All I meant was, I'll think about what I need to do . . . What are you going to do with all of those goodies?"

"My friend is coming over to pick me up for an early lunch. We'll drop everything off at the homeless shelter before my shift."

"Would you please leave a few things for me?"

"Help yourself."

I got up from the table, selected my share of goodies, set the platter down on my grandmother's sideboard, and looked at Kate.

"Aren't you going to ask me about last night?"

"Would you tell me the truth if I did?"

I hesitated, "I don't know."

"Well, when you do know, we'll talk about it. If you can't be honest with me, don't waste my time." Turning her back on me,

Kate slammed her fist into a bowl of dough and began kneading another loaf of bread.

I poured a glass of juice, selected a pastry, and started to leave the kitchen.

Kate crossed the room, gestured at the newspaper, "Don't forget this. You have an assignment, remember?"

I slipped the newspaper under my arm and left the kitchen without another word. Upstairs, I checked my phone. Miles had texted *R U OK?* I didn't know, so I didn't answer. I put everything down on the small table and dropped into my comfy armchair, but found no comfort. I finished the pastry, washing it down with the last of the juice, and picked up the newspaper. The headlines warned of another tropical storm ramping up, with landfall expected by nightfall or early morning. More rain meant more humidity, if that were even possible. It was relentless! How do people live here? This place makes Alabama seem downright comfortable.

Angry, I threw the newspaper across the room. Now what? I hated to admit it, but Kate was right. I had brought constant chaos into her world. There was little or no chaos in my world before Dad died and now there's nothing but. I wondered how much more could I take.

Marguerite might be right. Perhaps I did need a spiritual cleansing. *Should I go to the spiritual cleansing ceremony tonight? If there is even a remote possibility of contacting my father, I absolutely must go. I need to say "goodbye" to my dad. I need to find peace. This ceremony is my only hope.*

I had to focus. *If I were to go to the ceremony tonight, how would I get there? Marguerite said she would meet us at the dock. How am I supposed to make that happen? I can't rent a car. I can't ask Miles to take me. That's never going to happen. If by some miracle I could get a car, should I go get Angel? Marguerite said to bring her, but it might not be a good thing for Angel. But, then again, what could it hurt? I could use some company, even if she is younger than me. Should I tell her about us possibly being related? If so, what and how much should I tell her? I should probably tell her everything. But, then again, maybe not.* I put my head in my hands—I was making myself crazy.

Damn you, Dad, how could you leave me like this?

Was there any conceivable way for me to get to that ceremony tonight? My mind was scrambling to work out a plan when I heard footsteps coming up the sidewalk. I hurried to the window and drew the delicate lace aside. Kate's friend was here to pick her up; they wouldn't be here long. I had my plan. If her spare car key was hanging in the butler's pantry, I could just borrow the Mini, go get Angel, go get "spiritually cleansed," and be back before Kate got home from work. It was a simple, straightforward plan, almost elegant. And it could work. *Should I text Miles and tell him, so at least somebody knows my plan? Better not. He'll just get mad. He'll try to talk me out of it. Or worse, he'll tell his dad, who would call Kate. What a disaster that would be.*

I booted up my laptop and MapQuested the route to Angel's house. I retrieved Marguerite's note, reread the directions to the dock, and calculated a timeline. *Thirty minutes to Angel's house, maybe another thirty minutes to talk to her about our family. Maybe we'll take Gumbo for a walk so we can speak privately. That should work. It will take at least an hour to get to the dock. If I leave here around 4:30, I will have plenty of time. A cleansing ceremony can't take very long, right? I'll be back well before Kate gets home. If I fill up the car with gas on the way back, she'll never even know I was gone. Perfect! Just perfect!*

What does one wear to a spiritual cleansing ceremony? Should I wear the dress that Marguerite gave me? Maybe a turban? After all, I do have quite the ancestry for this sort of thing. Nah, I think I'll go as is, shorts, tee shirt, and sandals. It's too hot for anything else.

I passed the time by surfing the Net. No current events were particularly exciting and nothing held my interest. I decided to look up *spiritual cleansing ceremony*, but found nothing that gave any indication as to what I should expect this evening. I did, however, learn how many New Age, tree-hugging bloggers were out there leading the spiritual cleansing charge. Marguerite was not one of those people. She was definitely a woman of mystery. Harmless? Dangerous? I supposed the answer depended on who was offering an opinion. To date, she had been kind to me and interested. That's all I cared about.

Kate called up the stairs, "We're leaving now. I'll be home around ten thirty or so. Remember, you are *grounded*. Stay home and stay out of trouble."

I came out of my room, leaned over the railing, waved the newspaper at her, and said, "No problem. Have a nice time! Bye!"

As soon as they drove off, I threw the newspaper back in my room and ran downstairs to see if the spare set of keys was still hanging in the pantry. Bingo! I slipped the key ring into my pocket and ran back upstairs to get my purse, my cell, and the directions. I was on my way out when it occurred to me that I could use some of the fresh baked goods as a gift for Angel's mother. Simone wouldn't question why I was out there by myself if I was simply being neighborly. I picked a pastry box from the shelf, loaded it up with goodies, and tied a pink satin ribbon around it for good measure.

Excited at the prospect of bringing my chaos to an end, my heart raced as I pulled away from the curb. I inched the Mini through the French Quarter until, finally, the traffic ground to a halt. A wedding parade, led by a jazz band, danced away from St. Louis Cathedral on their way to the soon-to-be-raucous wedding reception. Guests had already armed themselves with red plastic cups filled to the brim with indeterminate alcoholic beverages.

They twirled their way through the streets as if nobody else or what they needed to do mattered.

I glanced at my watch; the clock was ticking. I needed to get Angel and get to the dock, before I quite literally missed the boat. As the last of the revelers passed in front of my car and the music faded into the early evening, I hit the gas and sped out of the Quarter. Already off schedule, I hoped I could make up the time to get to the Ninth Ward, even though I'd never found it on my own before.

I stopped at a light, quickly reread the directions, I was on track. I hadn't yet made a wrong turn.

Chapter Twenty-One

As I made my way closer to the Ninth Ward, I was overwhelmed by a sense of foreboding. The sky had turned a sort of yellow-gray, with skyscraper-sized clouds. The wind gusted, rocking the Mini. I tried to shake off the bad feeling by rationalizing that it was caused by a change in barometric pressure from the next storm headed our way. It was nothing more than that. Angel and I would be back home, safe and sound, well before the weather became hideous and anyone realized we were gone.

I stopped the Mini in front of Angel's house, removed the pastry box from the seat, and went to find her. I didn't have to look very hard. The screen door slammed open and Angel flew out, with Gumbo on her heels. Simone watched from the doorway, smiling when she saw me with the pretty pink pastry box.

"Why, honey, you didn't need to bring us anythin'."

"Kate and I wanted you to have these. She was in a frenzy this morning, a baking frenzy that is, and she sort of overdid it. She baked way too many sweets for us. We wanted to share them with you, so here I am! Aunt Kate sends her regrets, she had to work." A perky smile lit up my face.

"Mighty nice of her to let you drive her fine car. Sit yourself down, I'll get us some sweet tea."

"Thank you for asking, but I don't care for any tea. I thought maybe Angel and I could take Gumbo for a walk, spend some time together? That is, if you're okay with it, ma'am." Charm simply oozed from my lips.

"Don't think so, a storm is comin' in."

"Please Mama? We won't go far. Promise." Angel crossed her heart and said, "Scout's honor."

"Just up the block," said Simone. "I've gotta get the wash off the line before the storm comes up. Can't you hear the flappin' comin' from the back? The sheets have gotta be dry by now!" she laughed.

Angel hooked Gumbo up to his new leash and off we went.

I glanced at my watch again. "Angel, we need to talk."

"About what?"

"About us. You and me."

"Me and you? Why?"

"We're cousins. You and I are cousins."

Angel pulled on Gumbo's leash to stop him. She stared at me and began to laugh.

"You're funny. Look at me, I'm not white like you and you're not black like me. You're crazy girl, you wound those curls on your head too tight today."

"I'm serious. You know that picture of your maw-maw? I found one just like it in a box of our family photos. I thought she was a maid or something, but when I asked Kate, she said she wasn't a servant, she was family. A well-kept family secret is how she put it. She's my maw-maw, too!"

"Huh? How's that work?"

"It works through mixed-race relationships. Sexual relations between different races can change the dominant race. Look Angel, we don't have time to go into our family genealogy. We have to leave. We can talk about it in the car."

"Gene-ology? What's that? What's up with you, girl? Go where?"

"To the swamp. To the spiritual cleansing ceremony. Marguerite said you should be there. I don't want to go alone anyway. Please come with me. I need you. I'll take Gumbo, put him in your room and close the door. I'll go say goodbye to your mom. You go hide in the car."

"I can't. I've never lied to my mama before. I told her we'd be right back."

"She won't even know you're gone. We won't be long. I promise," I said, crossing my heart. "Scout's honor."

"I do wanna ride in her car!" Angel giggled, "Okay, I'll go!"

I gave her a little push towards the car and took the leash, then went back inside the house and closed Gumbo in Angel's room. I walked through the kitchen to the backyard, found Simone and told her that Angel was tired after our walk and wanted to take a little nap. I said "Goodbye" and headed for the car. I was dripping with sweat and wished I'd brought towels to cover Kate's nice leather seats. I hated sticking to car seats; it was such a pain. I looked at the sky again, now more charcoal than yellow-gray. I needed to put the car top up anyway, so when I turned on the A/C, the car would be more comfortable. I turned the car around and parked down the block, out of view from Angel's house. Angel and I struggled against the wind to close the canvas top. Finally, we were on our way.

I hesitated, unsure how to ask the next question.

"Angel, you can read, right?"

"What kind of fool question is that? Course I can read. What's got into you today? You're actin' all weird."

"Oh, I am so sorry! I didn't see a school in your neighborhood, so I figured . . ."

"We've got these big yellow things called buses, they get us to school." Angel gave me the stink-eye.

Ashamed, I said, "That *was* rude of me. I apologize. Let me start over. Would you please read the directions for me?"

"Maybe."

"Please, Angel?"

"You've gotta tell me how we're cousins, it makes no sense to me."

"I'll try to explain, as best I can, but help me get out of the city first."

We both fell silent.

"You know, Angel, I don't understand any of this myself. It's all news to me. I haven't wrapped my head around it yet. I'm hoping Marguerite can help. Or maybe you and I can figure it out together. You'd like that wouldn't you?"

"Who's that?"

"She's a woman I know. Sort of. She's a Voodoo high priestess, she understands these things. I believe she can help us."

"Voodoo priestess? Like my, uh, our maw-maw? That's cool! My mama says Voodoo isn't anything more than a different kind of religion. My mama and me, we're Baptist, but she told me maw-maw was Catholic and a Voodoo. I don't get how that works."

"Angel, where do I go from here? I've never been outside of New Orleans, have you?"

"I got an uncle that lives out the swamp. We go fishin' sometimes and he lets me drive his boat. Don't tell my mama, she says I'm too young yet to run a boat."

"I thought you said you didn't lie to your mama?"

"It's not lying if you just don't say anythin', right?"

"Right!"

Another gust of wind pushed against the Mini. I fought for control as we crossed the canal that flowed into Lake Pontchartrain. Again, silence filled the car. We both looked at the levees and thought about the tropical storm heading our way.

"April?"

"Yes?"

"You sure about this? Goin' to the swamp mightn't be a good idea."

"We'll be fine. We'll do this ceremony thing, hop back in the car and get home before the storm makes landfall. Don't worry, I'll take care of you."

"You need to get on the causeway, that'll get us to the swamp. Mama told me once it's the longest bridge in the world. I was scared first time I rode over it, but I was just a little kid back then. Nothin' but water and bridge, water and bridge, water and bridge. Pretty scary."

That didn't sound too good to me either, but I had to get to the swamp. There was no other route except across that bridge.

Angel looked out of the car window and said, "My mama told me after Hurricane Katrina, lots of places out here were left to just die." She pointed out the window, "See over there? The Six Flags Jazzland, that's one of them. Mama told me she went there once."

I glanced out her window at the skeletons of roller coasters and other monstrous park rides half hidden under mountains of weeds, where the laughter and amusement had long since died. I imagined on days like this or on full moon nights, the ghosts of enjoyment past could still be heard echoing in the gloom.

I turned on the radio. Every station warned their listeners to "batten down the hatches." The commentators tried to be light, but serious. Everyone was on edge, especially me. As we drove onto the causeway, another blast of heavy wind tried to blow us into the wall. Angel screamed, grabbed for the dashboard and braced for collision. My heart pounded as I tightened my grip on the wheel and fought to bring the little car back under control.

"It won't be much longer," I told her. "We'll be off the bridge soon."

"Sign says the bridge is twenty-four miles long. That isn't soon."

Angel was right. We wouldn't be off the bridge soon. There was no way to go except forward. There was no way to turn back.

"Hang on tight, Angel!" I shouted as the wind pushed against the car again.

After what seemed like forever, the Mini rolled onto terra firma. I relaxed my grip on the steering wheel and began to breathe a little easier. Angel high-fived me, let out a nervous little laugh. "That was some ride! Man oh man."

The landscape changed to a lush, green marshy one that was quite beautiful to look at. The late afternoon sun escaped from behind an enormous cloud, its rays casting a golden-black glow over us. Maybe it was a sign that everything would be okay. I could use a good omen about now. I doubted that would be the case, though. I watched a flock of birds fly inland, away from the water and the gathering storm.

Angel pointed to a sign. "Here! Turn here. We're goin' to Prosper's Fish Camp."

I did as she said, made a sharp right turn onto a dirt road and slowed the Mini. In addition to a stop for gas, the car would need to be washed before going back to Kate's house.

"You sure you wanna do this, April? We can turn back 'n' go home right now."

"We can't do that now, Angel."

"Why?"

"That's why." I pointed towards the dock.

Standing on the dock, shrouded in the early evening mist, was Madame Marguerite, beckoning us to join her.

Chapter Twenty-Two

"Welcome, my girls." Marguerite's voice was quiet and smooth as silk. She leveled her pale gold gaze on my new cousin. "You must be Angel."

"Yes, ma'am," said Angel, retreating somewhat.

"Come, we must hurry. The hour is late, the ceremony will soon begin."

"I have to go," cried Angel. "Real bad." She crossed her legs for emphasis.

"Me, too," I said, now not so sure I wanted to be here.

Marguerite pointed to a nearby porta potty. "Over there. Make it quick. We must leave!"

Angel and I scurried over to the blue plastic rectangle.

Inside, the portable toilet was hot, airless, and suffocating, its tiny window covered by a broken screen. No air could get in, only flies and other creepy, crawly things, and they had all died in quiet desperation in the minuscule sink. The "odor absorbing" chemicals couldn't overcome the steamy stench. My head began to spin, I stumbled out the door, falling into Angel.

"Can we go home now?" she whined. "I'm scared."

I leaned close to Angel. "Me, too, Angel. Listen to me. I need to do this. My father's spirit needs to find peace. I need to find peace. Marguerite said she could help me. You know I can't leave you here, or in the car by yourself. You have to come with me. You have no choice. I promise I'll take care of you. Scout's honor."

Angel said nothing, just kicked at the dirt.

"Young ladies, come now!" ordered Marguerite.

Surreptitiously, I looked at my phone and was amazed to see full bars. Concerned by the low-battery indicator, I powered off the phone and slipped it into my pocket.

"We can wait no longer!" shouted Marguerite.

"Coming."

Angel had a death grip on my hand as we ran towards the boat, but I was not unhappy about it. I had a death grip on hers as well.

Marguerite cast off even before we planted ourselves on the bench in the middle of the boat. Two paddles lay at our feet and a large cage full of chickens had been secured to a hook at the front of the boat. *Chickens? What's that about? What on earth do chickens have to do with spiritual cleansing?* I glanced at my watch again. It was 7:30, thirty minutes before the start of the ceremony. If the ceremony started on time and didn't take too long, there would still be plenty of time to get gas, get the car washed, get Angel home, and get back myself before Kate returned. I should be good. Everything was going according to plan.

With Angel dead silent beside me and Marguerite busy piloting the boat, my mind wandered. I pushed aside any dark thoughts of what might be in store for us when we docked. I focused on anything and everything I could possibly absorb from this primeval paradise. Fascinated by the rich environment, I wished Miles were here to give another of his fabulous tour commentaries. This was a world I had never experienced before, but would like to know more about. It was quiet, peaceful, and dramatic in a tropical-rain-forest sort of way. Under any other circumstance, I would have a better appreciation for the verdant landscape.

The tiny, bright green plants that covered the water's surface slipped easily away as the boat moved through the everglade. Sage-green Spanish moss dripped from every tree branch and deep purple water lilies dotted the shoreline. A blue heron, a bird I'd only seen in *National Geographic*, perched on a partially submerged log, still as a garden statue. It was a beautiful canvas, a living Impressionist painting. The swamp air was heavier, more humid, even more oppressive than the city's. Steam rose from the water, giving the swamp a *Jurassic Park* feel.

I pointed to the shore. "Is that an alligator?"

"No, it's a log," Angel answered. "Gators don't come out before a storm. They go to where they feel safe. Nobody knows where the gators go, they just go. Smarter than you and me, they are."

Lost in the beauty of the swamp, I had forgotten about the impending storm. Out here, there were no big gusts of wind or threatening clouds, only the quiet passing from day to evening. *Is the storm moving back out into the Gulf?*

As we motored past, lights came on inside a ramshackle cabin. Weathered shanties and abandoned shacks lined the shore, nestled alongside brand new double-wide trailers balanced on stilts high above the water line. Some places were well kept, others not so much. I was surprised to see there was a community of sorts out here. People living in a swamp was something I hadn't ever thought about. Then again, why would I? This was all so foreign to me.

Old wringer wash tubs and ice boxes decorated yards, adding the flair of a junkyard sculpture garden to the neighborhood. Flat boats and the occasional fishing boat rocked idly at weathered docks. Some of the oldest buildings looked like they had been here since the Civil War. No matter how old or ugly their appearance was, none of the homes was without a satellite dish. It was amazing to me that the tentacles of technology had reached this remote place. My mind flashed on a bizarre new reality show, *Real Housewives of the Bayou*. Not a pretty picture.

We passed a weathered general store at Prosper's Fish Camp, where an old blue sign with icicle letters advertised *Refrigerated Air Inside*. A barrel of live bait and two sparkling vending machines crowded the sagging porch. I wondered how long it would be before everything fell in on itself and was swallowed up by the marsh, disappearing as if it had never existed in the first place. Daylight slowly faded as we motored on, deeper into the gloom.

"Not much farther, ladies," said Marguerite, cutting the motor and pulling it out of the water.

"Help me," she said, reaching for a paddle. "The roots from the cypress trees and the water plants, they grow too thick to motor in. We paddle from here."

The night was alive with insect song. Wildlife moved unseen through the trees; at least I hoped it was wildlife. I heard drums in the distance and saw a reddish glow above the tree tops. We were almost there.

We paddled to the shore, where Marguerite tied our boat to a low-lying dock in desperate need of repair. She hefted the old wooden cage full of protesting chickens, as if she had done this many times before.

Marguerite turned to us. "Follow me."

Angel gasped, held back, whispered to me, "April, this don't feel right. Even the chickens know this isn't right. How come you don't know this isn't right? Let her go ahead. We can take the boat and skedaddle on outta here."

"Angel, I need to do this. It won't be long now. Then we can go, I promise," I whispered back. "When the ceremony is over my father's spirit will rest easy for all eternity. Mine, too. I need this."

Angel bowed her head, muttered something I couldn't hear, and kissed the cross around her neck before we scampered after Marguerite up the overgrown path. The beauty of the swamp escaped me now. Branches slapped at my bare skin, tearing at my flesh. Countless insects buzzed and bit. Angel tripped over a root and cried out. I helped her up, looked her over, and found nothing broken, only skinned knees and elbows. Clearing our way through a tangle of vines, we neared the end of the rugged path. The drums grew louder; the bonfire crackled and popped as the dry wood ignited, turning the sky blood red. My heart raced as adrenaline pumped into my system. I hadn't known what to expect of a spiritual cleansing ceremony, but it certainly wasn't this. *Spiritual cleansing* sounded so gentle, almost baptismal.

Marguerite stopped. Angel and I watched as, with her head held high, Marguerite appeared to grow taller. With her regal silhouette illuminated by the glow of the bonfire, her entrance to the clearing was made that much more dramatic. We followed, but kept our distance. My heart felt like it would burst as I absorbed the spine-chilling tableau.

Three dreadlocked drummers (two of whom I recognized from the Voodoo shop) and more than two dozen devotees dressed in white encircled the clearing where an intense bonfire burned. Angel and I stayed on the sidelines while Marguerite made her way to the center. A painfully thin young man about Angel's age came forward; he wore no shirt or shoes. He bowed to Marguerite, took the cage and placed it near a tethered baby goat. The goat bleated at the squawking chickens. A greeting? Or plotting their escape? On the far side of the clearing was an older man, again without shoes or shirt, dancing, grinning, and twirling two gleaming machetes like some sort of maniacal drum major.

The drummers stopped. Marguerite circled around, her arms open wide, as if to embrace the dozens of devotees.

"Welcome my friends! We have gathered this evening to bring peace to those without peace. Tonight we come together to give safe passage to all wandering, restless souls." She held me with her gaze. "And, tonight we shall provide peace to another soul without anchor."

Angel gripped my hand tighter, moaned softly and shrunk into herself. The first drummer started a slow beat on his drum, then the second one started, and finally the third drummer joined the rhythmic thumping. Marguerite pulled a small muslin bag from her pocket. She opened it and began to place pinches of white corn meal in a circle around a tall cross-topped pole. She created an astral design (a *Veve*, she called it) used to invoke the spirits, the *Loa*. She circled again, added more white powder symbols to her design. She chanted quietly as she designed her way around the pole, like a sorceress working her black magic.

One by one, the crowd began to sway, chanting with Marguerite until they were in full chorus and writhing as one. The drum beat intensified. If the dead were not already restless, they soon would be. Angel stood quaking at my side.

I felt overwhelmed by the heat, the humidity, the noise, and the stunning realization that I had made a terrible mistake by coming here, especially by bringing Angel with me. *What have I done?*

I looked around the circle at the twisting, keening devotees. I looked at the twirling man, his chest now glistening with sweat, his machetes gleaming in the firelight. I looked at the little black and white goat and the chickens. Finally, I understood.

Sacrifice.

Before I could faint, I heard or felt from deep within, my father, as if he were standing right beside me, *"Get out of here now, April!"*

Feeling like I'd been punched in the gut was the jolt I needed. *Dad is still here for me! His spirit will always be with me, guiding me, protecting me.* And now, it was up to me to protect Angel before she became even more traumatized. But I had to get her out of the clearing first.

I tapped Angel's trembling shoulder. She looked up at me. Her bottom lip was quivering, her eyes as dilated as a drug addict's. She was more frightened than anyone I had ever seen. I felt horrible for what I had done to her. I held a finger to my lips and nodded towards the path. The devotees were so entranced, I doubted anyone would notice if we left. I drew Angel close to me and we began to slink away, one step backwards at a time. Abruptly, the drumming and chanting stopped. The shirtless man ceremoniously approached the blazing bonfire, crossed the glimmering machetes over his head and grinned like Batman's Joker.

Marguerite whirled around, pointed to me, and commanded, "Bring me the cage."

Chapter Twenty-Three

Everyone turned towards me, their eyes glowing red in the fire-light, ratcheting up the fear factor. If ever there was a time to make a run for it, it would be now.

But my feet wouldn't move.

Louder this time, Marguerite bellowed, "Bring me the cage."

Angel cried, "April, noooooo!" and tightened her grip on my shirt.

I looked around, realizing we were just as trapped as the animals. Seeing no other way out of this, I slowly moved forward. Angel pulled at my shirt, tried to bring me back.

"April, we gotta get out," Angel whispered. Desperately afraid, she began to cry.

I had no plan, but knew it was time to act. What could I possibly do to get this sorted out? I'd made such a mess of everything. I couldn't think about it now. Regrets could wait. I had to focus on the here and now, on Angel.

"Angel, I don't have a choice. Come with me, you can stand by the goat. Here, take my hand," I said, moving towards the chickens, my mind racing.

Angel gripped my hand and followed, sobbing as we worked our way closer to the animals. I looked back and saw that the man with the machetes had a fixed, menacing smile as he flashed his killing tools in anticipation.

"Angel, look. Look at that baby goat. She's frightened, just like you and me. Please stay with her, pet her, hug her. You can help her. She needs you," I said with as much calm as I could muster. I reached for the cage.

"April, I ca-can't. I ju-just can't do this," Angel stuttered, crying inconsolably.

Her agony broke my heart. I took Angel by the shoulders and lightly shook her. I looked deep into her eyes, "Angel, please stop crying! I need your help. The goat needs your help. I need you to take care of her. Do you understand me? Do you?"

Angel raised her head, looked at me, looked back at the goat. Her eyes grew wide.

"You understand me now, right, Angel?"

Angel nodded, wiped away the tears with the back of her hand and moved closer to the bleating baby goat. As Angel patted her, the little goat quieted. I picked up the cage, turned towards my audience, held my head high.

All eyes were on me now. I affected an air of great aplomb, as I'd seen the famous actresses, like Vivien Leigh, do in the classic movies I watched with my dad. I walked with grand ceremony into the arena. It was difficult to manage, as the cage was rocking with flapping, frightened chickens. I used that to my advantage, appearing to struggle mightily. As I approached the center of the circle, I stared intently at Marguerite, one unsteady step at a time.

Marguerite, arms stretched out towards the heavens, was bathed in an aura of firelight, her golden eyes burning as intensely as the bonfire.

She called out, "Now is the time to bring peace to the restless spirits. Oh, beautiful descendant of the great Queen Marie Laveau, come to me. Together we shall raise her *Loa*."

The drums began their beat once more, this time in sync; slowly at first, then faster and faster, driving the devotees into a whirling frenzy. One by one they fell to the ground moaning and writhing, as if possessed by angry demons. Lightning ripped across the starless night, thunder crashed in the distance.

"Bring me the cage, my child!" ordered Marguerite.

I stopped, looked squarely into her glowing, golden eyes. Inch by inch, I raised the cage as high as I could over my head.

"Not in this lifetime! And, Madame, *I am not your child!*"

When I let go, the cage hit the hard packed dirt with a loud crack, the old wooden sides split open and the chickens exploded into the night. Taking her cue, Angel unhitched the baby goat, wrapped her arms around its tiny belly and ran towards the edge of the clearing.

Machete Man dropped his gleaming instruments near the fire and began to chase the chickens. The devotees sprang into action, joining the chase. Everyone trampled the intricate Voodoo designs Marguerite had carefully crafted. The white powder dispersed, clouding the air. It was awesome chaos! The scene was totally like something out of an incredibly dark Marx Brothers movie. I would have laughed out loud if I could have.

I gave Marguerite one long, last parting look. She smiled briefly, nodded her head and turned her back on me.

Unsure exactly what she meant, but unwilling to stick around to find out, I swiftly crossed the clearing and ran to catch up with Angel. The nearly invisible path to the clearing was now completely invisible. I had no clue where we were or how to get back to the boat. Away from the bonfire light, I was cloaked by the inky black night. Disoriented and way out of my element, I had difficulty finding Angel.

I hissed, "Angel, where are you?"

"Here."

"Where?"

"By the tree."

What tree? There are thousands out here! I wanted to scream at her, but didn't.

"Hang on a second, Angel. There's a flashlight on the keychain."

I grabbed the keys from my pocket and, thank God, it was there. I shined the flashlight around until its narrow beam settled on two frightened figures crouched by a tree just ahead. As I got closer, I saw that a large spider's web had separated from the tree and wrapped Angel's shoulders like a delicate lace shawl. The web's gargantuan architect crawled cautiously down a branch towards Angel. I hated spiders—in fact, I loathed spiders. Spiders always scared the heck out of me, but Dad was always there to get rid of them. Now, it was my turn.

"Angel, don't move, honey. Stay where you are. I'm coming to get you," I said, looking around for something to use.

"*Bleat! Bleat!*"

"Was that you or the goat?" I laughed, trying to bring a little levity to the situation, keep Angel calm.

I dropped the light, grabbed a fallen branch, rushed full speed towards the tree and smacked the seemingly softball-sized arachnid into the air before it could do Angel any harm.

"What was that about?"

"Oh, nothing much. Just a little spider, that's all. It's gone now, not to worry," I said, doing a little victory dance.

I dropped the branch, retrieved the flashlight, reached down and wiped away the nasty web. I took the goat from Angel, held out my hand and helped her up.

"Time to go home, Angel. I think we've overstayed our welcome."

Angel grinned and rolled her eyes. We both jumped at the sound of someone or something crashing through the trees. I turned off the light and heard Angel gasp.

"You know this place is full of wild boars, right?"

"Pigs on steroids? Out here? In the swamp?"

"Yep! And meaner than all get out. Must've smelled Baby Goat here. They're thinkin' dinner."

"Baby Goat, let's get you outta here before anybody or anything else decides you'd make a tasty treat."

"*Bleat!*"

"My sentiments exactly."

Grateful that the goat was tiny, I hugged her close with one arm, like a four-legged, furry football. With my free hand, I shined the flashlight at our feet, moving its narrow beam back and forth, looking for any sign of the path. Nothing jumped out at me, which was probably a good thing, given the fact that this place was chock full of creepy, crawly, dangerous things and, of course, people. Lightning slashed the sky. The wind picked up, slowing our progress. The vicious storm brewing in the Gulf was headed our way. I closed my eyes for a moment, felt the hot wind on my skin. *Would the wind be blowing in from the water?*

The crashing grew louder. I heard hushed voices.

I whispered, "Angel, I don't know much about storms, but thinking logically—if I'm even capable of logic at the moment—maybe if we walk, or better yet run, into the wind, we'll come to the water and find the boat. It's worth a try anyway. For sure we can't turn back, that'll just take us into the path of those crazies. Let's move on."

I directed the light at our feet as we moved farther away from the clearing. Exactly where we were going, though, I had no clue. I hoped against hope we were headed in the right direction.

Chapter Twenty-Four

It was slow going for the three of us. Baby Goat, who forever after shall be known as BG, grew heavier with each step, but I couldn't leave her behind. The chickens—well, I was sorry for them, but I believed they had a better chance at escaping capture. At least, they could flap, claw, and peck at potential captors.

The rain hadn't started yet, but it wouldn't hold off much longer. The wind was stronger now; the thunder came faster after the lightning. Which wrath was going to be worse, Mother Nature's or Aunt Kate's? If I didn't make it home before she did, I'd put my money on Kate.

Angel had a tight grip on the back of my shirt, hanging on for dear life. We stumbled through tangles of trees, vines, and roots, swatted at unseen, bloodthirsty insects.

"Ouch!" Another branch grazed Angel's arm.

I stopped and turned the flashlight on Angel. Scratches and mosquito bites covered exposed skin from head to toe. Same for me. There would be no hiding the fact we had gone rogue.

"Angel, I am so sorry I got you into this mess. I don't know what I was thinking. I guess I wasn't thinking at all. I don't know if I can ever make this up to you or if your mother will ever forgive me. She must know by now that you aren't home. What have I done?"

"Because of you, my mama's gonna leash me up like Gumbo and never let me loose. Your auntie too, I betcha."

"You got that right. My days of freedom are over, no doubt about it. Which way should we go?"

"Keep goin' into the wind. We've gotta be gettin' close to the water," she answered.

I turned around, headed into the wind with Angel gripping my shirt. It seemed like hours, but only minutes had passed when we came upon a decaying cabin and a disintegrating dock. Bad luck, no boat. There was no way for me to tell if we were above or below the dock where Marguerite left her skiff. At least we had finally reached the shoreline. I didn't much care if we found her boat or not. At this point, any boat would suffice. I'd be happy to add boat theft to my ever-growing list of transgressions. I needed to get us out of here.

Right or left, left or right? The decision was made when I heard voices coming at us from behind and to our right. Left it was.

"Angel, hear that? It sounds like they're getting closer. I don't know if they're chasing us, or trying to get out of here themselves before the storm hits. Be as quiet as you can. Follow me."

As we worked our way down the shore, fat drops of rain began to fall. *Perfect, just perfect.* The ground beneath our feet quickly turned to mud. Our sandals made sucking sounds as we slogged along the shore. When lightning split the sky, I could see Marguerite's boat just ahead.

I whispered, "Angel, look! It's our boat. Can you run?"

"Maybe."

"Let's get outta here!"

Running through the mud wasn't easy, but we did it. Angel settled in the boat with BG while I untied the craft. I threw the rope to her.

"Tie BG up to the hook near the front. I need your help paddling out of here."

Angel looped the rope around BG, securing her to the hook. I pushed the boat away from the dock, took one of the oars, and gave the other one to Angel. We were on our way.

I always believed animals had better sense than people, especially me at the moment. My belief was confirmed as BG lay down in the front of the boat, curled into a little ball, and tucked her tiny legs under her belly, trying to avoid the rain. Our trip back to the other dock and the Mini was going to be significantly more difficult with a storm fighting our progress.

The wind whipped at our small boat as we paddled, hopefully in the right direction. It was taking all of my strength; it was doubtful that Angel would last much longer. I was quite proud of her. She hadn't fallen apart no matter how frightened she was. If truth be told, Angel did better than me. She had tried to talk me out of this "adventure," but I wouldn't listen.

No doubt about it, I'd been totally reckless. *Oh, my God, Marguerite's Tarot card reading was right! I have made reckless decisions and I have faced challenges. And, I'm still facing them! To make matters worse, I dragged Angel along for my ride! Oh-my-God-oh-my-God-oh-my-God! What have I done?* I put my mental brakes on. This was no time for self-flagellation. There would be plenty of time for that later.

We had only the flashlight and intermittent light from the homes on the shore to guide us through the storm to our dock. We paddled hard, fighting our way clear of tree roots and logs to more open water. Time to start the motor. I yanked the cord, got only a sputter. I yanked again—another sputter. With every ounce of remaining strength I had, I yanked a third time; the motor caught. We took off with a jerky start. I'd never piloted a boat before, and it wasn't as easy as it looked. I had real trouble getting my sea legs.

Over the raging wind, Angel hollered, "Hey, city girl, you ever done this before?"

"Never!"

"Move over. Let me do this. I can get us outta here."

I handed the tiller over to Angel, moved out of her way and withdrew my cell phone from my pocket to see if I had reception. I turned the phone back on; amazingly, it had bars. There were several texts and voicemails from Miles, even more from Kate. She wanted to know where I was, if I had seen Angel. Simone had called to say her daughter was missing, she had called the police.

Oh-my-God-oh-my-God-oh-my-God! I started a text: *Angel with me. Don't worry. Coming home.* But before I could hit SEND, my bad luck kicked into overdrive. Our boat ran over a log and the phone, slick with rain, flew from my hand and disappeared into the churning swamp.

Heavy rain started to fill the bottom of the small boat, adding the very real danger of sinking to our escape. Drenched and windblown, BG was probably scared out of her little goat mind, but she was mercifully quiet. I turned my face into the squall and spotted a hazy light up ahead. I prayed it was the right wharf and that we'd be in the car, on our way home, soon. It was.

A fierce blast of wind slammed the boat against the piling as Angel tried to dock. Struggling to balance myself, I held on to the rotting wood as I worked to tie up the boat. Mission accomplished. I untied the soaking wet BG, tucked her under my arm and scrambled up the small dockside ladder after Angel. Spent from the physical and emotional rollercoaster ride, Angel sat down and cried. I helped her to her feet with my free hand.

"Angel, you did great! Your uncle would be so proud of you! I certainly am!" I wrapped my arm around the shivering, sobbing child. "Come on, let's go. We need to get out of here."

Angel snuggled close as we hobbled against the wind and rain to the car. I opened the door, buckled BG into the back and watched in horror as the soaked goat pooped on the soft black leather seat. *Perfect! Just perfect!*

Angel climbed into the front seat, buckled up, and leaned against her headrest. The last one in, I took a minute, closed my eyes and thanked the universe for leading us back to the right dock. I buckled up, started the car, threw it in reverse, skidded against the wet gravel, and headed away from Prosper's Fish Camp.

All I wanted was to be back at Kate's house, cozied up in my nice four-poster bed, wearing dry clothes, with tonight behind me like a bad dream instead of the living nightmare it still was.

There would be no stop for either gas or car wash. There was no getting Angel back home without her mother finding out. There was no getting back home without Kate knowing. None of the things I had planned or thought would be simple had worked out, not by any stretch of the imagination.

There would be absolute hell to pay when I got us back to The Big Easy.

Chapter Twenty-Five

Except for providing directions back to the city, Angel was silent on the car ride home. I didn't much feel like talking either. I had some serious thinking to do. Would it be possible to spin this? Make it look not so hideous? Doubtful. Both of us were drenched, wounded, and worn out from the ordeal. Angel was sneezing and shivering; I hoped she wasn't getting sick, but knew she was. I didn't feel so good myself. The near-hurricane had ended and moved away from us. However, a Category 5 storm named Kate lay just down the road, waiting for my return.

Let me review. *What exactly did I do today? Nothing good, that's for sure. I lied to Kate about staying home and then I stole her car. I lied to Simone and then I took her daughter into a dangerous situation. I'd turned off my phone, something Kate had specifically asked me not to do ever again. Then, I lost the phone in the swamp, so nobody could track the GPS. Angel had been reported missing and now the police were involved. That pretty much sums up most, but not all of my day. Oh yeah, and how was I going to explain the goat? Gee, Kate, what was I supposed to do, let Machete Man sacrifice BG to the Loa? That alone would most definitely invite a whole new round of questions and criticisms, not that it would be unjustified. In hindsight, I had not used good judgment. Or any judgment at all, for that matter. Quite simply put, I was screwed and I had done it to myself.*

Where should I take Angel? If I take her home, I will have to explain everything to the police, who were probably at the house waiting with Simone. If I take Angel to Kate's house, I will have to explain everything to Kate. Police or Kate? Kate or police? What kind of trouble will I encounter if I go directly to Angel's house? Is Kate's house the lesser of two evils? Kate won't be in any frame of mind to help me, but she might want to help Angel.

I looked over at my new cousin. Angel was dozing with her head resting on the door. She looked younger and more fragile than she had earlier today. I hoped I hadn't scarred her for life with this *misadventure* of mine. Everyone had hunkered down for the storm. There was no traffic to speak of and I made good time driving back to the city.

"Angel, wake up. I need your help to get through the city and back to Kate's house. I don't know where I'm going."

"I wanna go home. You said you'd get me home before my mama knew I was gone," said Angel in a soft, sleepy voice.

"Well, honey, I think your mama already knows you're gone. She called Kate. I think it will be better if Kate takes you home."

"What! When? Gimme your phone. I wanna call Mama and let her know I'm okay," cried Angel.

"Uh, I lost my phone in the swamp. We'll be at Kate's in a few minutes, you can call her from there."

"You lied! You said everything would be okay, we'd get back before my mama knew. You lied to me and now I'm gonna get in trouble because of you. You're a bad, bad girl."

"I'm sorry, Angel. I can't tell you how sorry I am that I got us into this mess. You're right, everything is my fault and I don't know how to fix it. I don't think I can."

Of course Angel was right. *I am a bad, bad girl. Exactly when did I go wrong?* I was pretty sure I'd have plenty of time to reflect on my horrible self later, but first, I needed to get Angel to Kate's, then back home to her mother. Angel didn't speak again except to direct me through the city. When we got to Jackson Square, I knew it wouldn't be much longer.

"Um, Angel . . . I have one last favor to ask of you . . . would you mind not telling . . ."

Angel turned and stared at me in disbelief.

"Never mind, forget I asked. I'll figure something out."

I was two blocks from Kate's house when I spotted red and blue flashing lights reflecting off of rain-streaked windowpanes and pavement. I slowed the Mini. At the bottom of the next block I could see several police cars, a big, black SUV with tinted windows and a NOPD K9 unit van. Everyone was milling around, speaking rapidly into walkie-talkies. It looked like they were in the throes of organizing a manhunt or an Amber Alert or something. I looked past the vehicles. Kate was speaking to Detective Baptiste, who was totally in command of the situation. Miles stood on the porch holding Simone's hands, trying to comfort her. Gumbo barked frantically at a bloodhound, probably Miles's dog Nosey, who paid him no mind. The German shepherds sat still, silently waiting for their orders.

Oh, I am so busted.

Angel's eyes grew wide. "Mama! There's my mama! Oh, I'm gonna get it for sure. And, you . . . you're gonna get it, too. Your auntie's lookin' a lot like those chickens in the swamp, all flappin' mad."

Angel was right again. No doubt about it, Kate looked flappin' mad.

"Okay, Angel, this is it. I'll park as close as I can to the house. We'll walk the rest of the way. Let me do the talking."

"April, I'm scared!" Her little voice quivered.

"Me, too, honey. Me, too!"

I lowered each of the windows a bit to give BG some air. I thought it best if we just left her in the car for the time being. Angel and I got out of the Mini and headed for the house. Gumbo alerted to us first and loped down the block to greet us. One by one, all heads turned in our direction. Pandemonium erupted as everyone realized we had returned.

Simone flew after Gumbo. Kate, Miles, and Detective Baptiste followed closely behind. Simone scooped Angel into her arms, nearly hugging the life out of her, before the scolding began. Kate marched over to me. We eyed each other guardedly; neither one of us spoke. There would be no hug for me as Kate pulled her arm back, ready to slap. I braced myself for the hit, but the hit never came.

Kate was stopped mid-slap by Detective Baptiste, who said, "Don't make this any worse than it already is."

Kate nodded, dropped her hand, and moved away from me and over to speak to Simone and Angel. At a complete loss for words, she turned and walked away.

Detective Baptiste pulled a female officer aside and brought her over to Simone and Angel. "Simone, this is Officer Jordan. I want you to go with her to the emergency room to get Angel checked out. I'll come by later for her statement."

He turned to Miles, "Take April inside and wait for us in the kitchen."

As Miles silently guided me towards the house, I watched as the NOPD officers turned off their flashing lights and left. The K9 unit officers bundled their German shepherds into the van and followed the police cruisers. Two indifferent FBI agents spoke briefly to Detective Baptiste, got into their black SUV, and sped off into the night.

Inside with Miles, there was nothing to say. I had no reasonable explanation for him or anybody else. At best, my behavior was wildly irrational. I didn't understand it myself.

Miles grabbed a hand towel from the powder room. "Dry off."

"I'll be right back, I'm going to get into some dry clothes," I said, heading for the stairs.

Miles took my arm and stopped me. "No, you're not. Dad said to wait in the kitchen. That's where we'll be when he comes in. I'm not sure you can be trusted to come back if I let you go upstairs."

Without any protest, I let Miles lead me into the kitchen to wait.

Chapter Twenty-Six

I took a seat at the kitchen table. Miles crossed the room and leaned against the counter. I couldn't bear to look at him. I was too ashamed. I kept my eyes lowered and stared at the floor. I felt his gaze burning from across the room. He didn't say a word. His silence was deafening, even more so than if he'd yelled at me.

"Miles, I, uh . . ."

"No, don't. Don't say a word."

"There's a goat in the car," I blurted.

"*What?*"

"There's a baby goat in the back seat of Kate's car. She can't stay there. Would you please go get her? Please?" I begged, taking the keys from my pocket and sliding them across the table.

He huffed, grabbed the key ring, pointed at me, and said, "Stay put."

I got up, took a bottle of cold water from the fridge, headed to the powder room and locked the door. I was a sight. Red, bumpy mosquito bites were crisscrossed by long scratches along my forehead and cheeks. My hands, shoulders, arms, and legs had also taken quite a beating from Mother Nature. There were bits and pieces of twigs, leaves, and even some sticky spider's web clinging to my curls. I took a long pull of the cold water, filled the sink with the rest and lowered my face into the frigid water, hoping to find some relief. The icy water felt like fire on my skin. I gingerly dried my damaged skin and finger-combed the odd bits of stuff from my hair. I unlocked the door, went back to the kitchen, and sat, anxiously awaiting my fate. I heard the front door open.

Kate, Detective Baptiste, Miles, and the click-click of goat's hooves headed my way. All eyes were on me as they entered the room, even BG, who looked confused.

"*Bleat!*"

"Where should I put the goat?" asked Miles.

Kate looked at the dripping goat and grabbed a handful of kitchen towels. She threw them to Miles and pointed at the door.

"Take the goat out to the sun porch and dry it off. There should be a blanket out there."

"Wait outside, Miles. I need to get April's statement," Detective Baptiste added.

"But, Dad, I need to hear this, too. I'll just stand over there in the corner. I'll stay quiet, I won't say a word."

"Sorry, Son, this is a police matter. April has rights. As her legal guardian, Kate will stay during questioning."

I looked up and searched Miles's face, desperately seeking an ally, but found none. He threw me a hard look before leading the goat from the kitchen.

My heart stopped. *Police matter?* Did I hear Detective Baptiste correctly?

"I'm going to read you your rights now, April. Please let me know if there is anything you do not understand. After the Miranda warning, you'll need to take us through today's events from the beginning."

I stared at Kate. She said nothing. She hadn't said a word to me since I returned. This was so much worse than I could have possibly imagined.

"I'm being *arrested*?" I asked, in a very small voice.

"Not yet. However, if either Kate or Simone decides to press charges, I will have no choice but to arrest you," he replied without emotion.

"Charges?" I whispered.

"Joyriding at the very least. Quite possibly grand theft auto."

Kate stood stone-faced across the room.

"You could also be charged with reckless child endangerment or kidnapping."

My stomach churned like the swamp as the grim reality sank in.

"Some of these charges are misdemeanors, others felonies. In the worst-case scenario, you could be facing felony charges and prison time, a fine as well. As arresting officer, it is up to me to identify the charges, but the district attorney will have final approval. Because it's an election year, the DA could decide to make an example of you as part of his 'tough on crime campaign.'"

"I'm gonna be sick." Racing from the kitchen, I made it to the powder room just in time. I heaved and heaved and heaved and passed out on the cool tile floor.

When I opened my eyes again, Kate was sitting in a chair in the corner of the room, a hospital room. It was morning already. Brilliant sunlight streamed through a window, warming my groggy head. I struggled to sit up.

"How are you feeling?"

"Thirsty," I squeaked. "What am I doing here?"

Kate rose to get some water. "You hit your head on the sink when you passed out. You have a concussion. You're also pretty sick with some weird swamp virus or a reaction to a spider bite. The test results aren't back yet. Angel is just down the hall with the same thing."

"Am I arrested?"

"No. Not yet anyway. You passed out before Detective Baptiste could read you your rights or get your statement. Fainting last night worked in your favor. Angel told us her version of what happened, but that doesn't mean you're off the hook. This is far from over. You need to understand there are consequences for your actions. How severe they are, is yet to be determined. Detective Baptiste still needs to take your statement and still needs to speak with Simone about charges. She wasn't up to talking last night. He and I need to discuss charges as well."

I averted my gaze, began twisting the sheet. I was speechless.

Kate continued, "I haven't quite decided what I want to do with you. The doctor recommended a psychologist for you."

"But . . ." I began to protest.

"April, don't even bother. You aren't in a position to whine or complain about anything. Consider yourself lucky you aren't already handcuffed to that bed. Trust me, last night I felt like handcuffing you until the day you turn eighteen, when you would be free to go and do as you please. And another thing, I've locked up your driver's license and my spare keys."

The nurse came in to check my vitals and draw more blood—like the mosquitoes hadn't taken enough last night.

Kate stood. "I'm going home to shower and change. I've been here all night. I'll be back later today. I need to be here when Detective Baptiste speaks with you. Just so you know, April, he got one of his colleagues to sit outside your door. Don't even think about going to see Angel or leaving the hospital. You can't see Angel until you give your statement. Even then, I'm not sure that Simone will let you near her. Get some rest while I'm gone. You're going to need it."

"Wait! Where's BG?"

"Who's BG?"

"Baby Goat. Is she okay?"

"She's fine. She's tethered in my courtyard. She'll stay there until I can figure out what to do with her."

Kate opened the door to leave.

"Aunt Kate?"

Kate turned around. "Yes?"

"Thank you."

"Don't thank me yet. You and I have a long way to go before we get this sorted out. Chances are you're not going to be happy with the results." Kate left the room, the door closing softly behind her.

I threw back the blanket, swung my legs over the side of the bed, and went into the tiny bathroom. Feeling lightheaded and unstable, I gripped the handicap bar next to the toilet. I glanced in the mirror, but had to turn away. I looked as horrible as I felt. My head ached, my scratches were sore, and the mosquito bites itched like crazy. I was in a fine mess and looked it. I made my way back to the bed, slipped between the stiff, starched sheets and tried to process everything that was happening.

Prison time.

Prison was a real possibility. Maybe if I showed remorse, everyone would go easy on me. That's how it always worked on television. But this definitely wasn't some scripted TV drama, this was my very own horrible personal drama. This was real. I couldn't be more remorseful. Or scared. I'd only been in New Orleans a few days, and in that short time, I'd managed to disappoint, hurt, or alienate everyone who tried to help me.

If life had a rewind button, I would do things differently. At least I hoped I would. But who knew? I didn't know myself anymore. Dad didn't raise me to behave so badly, to lie or steal or hurt people. Maybe the doctor was right. Maybe some counseling is in order. And from what Kate said, I didn't have a choice.

I got back into bed and rang for the nurse. I needed something to help with the headache and the itching and the nausea, which had returned. She brought some ointment for the mosquito bites, two tablets for my headache and crackers for the nausea. After she left, I located the remote and channel surfed. I had hoped for a little respite, but there was no escaping the voices in my head. I turned off the television.

I couldn't leave my room. I couldn't visit Angel. I was more or less under house arrest. With nobody to talk to and without the television to distract me, I closed my eyes and reviewed the previous day's events. I came to the conclusion that I had quite a few reasons to be worried about what the afternoon held for me. There was no way for me to know what Angel told everyone. When Detective Baptiste and Kate came back, I needed to be honest for once and tell them exactly what happened and why. My future depended on it.

No more secrets, no more lies.

Chapter Twenty-Seven

I didn't know what time it was when Kate and Detective Baptiste came back, but it didn't matter. It was time to get it over with.

"Hi," I said quietly as I sat up and they sat down.

"Are you feeling better? Do you feel up to doing this?" he asked.

"I guess so. Do you want to take notes or should I write everything down, like they do on TV? Do you have a pen and pad?"

Detective Baptiste pulled out a recorder, turned it on and set it on the hospital tray table. He read me my rights and asked if I understood them.

Scared out of my mind, I nodded and said, "Yes."

"Why don't you start at the beginning, take us through the events?"

And, that's exactly what I did. I talked for what seemed like hours. Once I started, I couldn't shut up. I told them everything I could think of, starting with the sudden death of my father and how I never got to say goodbye. I told them that since his passing, I had become more and more obsessed with saying good-bye. I convinced myself that Dad's spirit was as unsettled as mine. I thought I'd found the perfect solution in Marguerite and her spiritual cleansing ceremony. All I ever wanted was to find a final peace for both him and me. I told Detective Baptiste and Kate that I never intended to hurt Angel in any way. The only reason I took her with me was because I was afraid to go alone. The only reason I borrowed Kate's car was to get to the swamp for the

159

Voodoo ceremony. I didn't put any blame on Angel or Marguerite or anyone else. Everything that had happened was my doing. I didn't try to minimize it.

By the time I reached the end, I was worn out and my head was throbbing. There wasn't much left to say, except that I was terribly sorry for the turmoil I had caused. Before stopping completely, I added one last thing. I hoped they believed the experience had left an indelible impression on me, that I had learned from it. I was, without question, remorseful. I left out the part about being scared out of my mind that I might end up in juvie or, worse, prison.

Detective Baptiste turned off the recorder, slipped it back into his pocket and stood.

"Thank you, April. Get some rest."

He nodded at Kate and they both left the room. Thirty excruciatingly long minutes later, Kate returned alone.

"Where's Detective Baptiste?"

"He went down the hall to speak with Simone. To see if she still wants to press charges."

"Are you going to press charges?" I asked in a tiny voice.

I wanted to hear it from her, not Detective Baptiste.

Kate looked long and hard at me before answering. I was so panicked, I stopped breathing.

Finally, she answered, "No. I'm not pressing charges. After you've recovered from the virus and the concussion, you won't be on court-mandated probation, but you will be on Kate-mandated probation. You will go to counseling. You will get a job. You will do community service at a facility of my choosing. You will either walk or take a trolley wherever you need to go. You will pay for your replacement phone and you will keep it turned on at all times. And, you'll need to pay me back for the detail of my car. Understood?"

I nodded vigorously. "Understood. When do I get to go home?"

"Both you and Angel will get released after the doctor completes his workup, probably sometime tomorrow. I'll bring clean clothes for you in the morning."

"Aunt Kate?"

"Yes?"

"Why aren't you pressing charges?"

Kate dragged the chair close to the bed and sat down. "When I found out you not only stole my car but took Angel with you, my mind was made up. I didn't know what my legal options were, but if I could press charges, I definitely would. I was over the moon angry with you. I wanted to punish you. You know I never wanted children; your recklessness, your selfishness absolutely validated that decision. Last night, in the thick of the drama, I was really glad I never had kids of my own."

I slid lower in the bed, pulled the covers up under my chin.

"After you hit your head and were brought to the hospital, I sat here, watching you all night, worried sick. What you did was horribly deceitful and, without question, quite stupid, but prison time seemed extreme to me. I decided not to press charges unless you lied to us and your account of yesterday's events didn't match up with what we had already learned from Angel. In that case, I was fully prepared to let you go to jail."

Flashing on a picture of me in an orange prison jumpsuit, I quickly filed the image away in the "don't even go there" part of my brain.

Kate continued, "I'm not quite sure you fully appreciate how fortuitous it was that you needed to be hospitalized. It gave me time to evaluate the situation and consider my options. It would have been easiest for me if you had ended up in prison for a year or so. You would simply go away and I wouldn't have to deal with you any longer. Whenever you got released, you would be of age and could go forth into the world, be on your own."

I shrunk at the thought, pulled the covers tighter.

"But sometime during the middle of the night, I realized my decision shouldn't be about what was easiest for me. My decision should be about what is best for you. Call me crazy, but I honestly don't think you're a bad person, just seriously misguided. More than anything, you need stability, structure, and guidance. You need to know someone cares about you. You need someone that won't leave you. To the best of my ability, I'm going to try to do all of that for you. Understand me, though, you *will* be required to do your part. I am not in this alone. We are in this together."

I studied Kate's face and saw the weariness. She seemed to have aged years in the days since my arrival. As more appropriate words failed me, I simply said, "Thank you."

The door opened and Detective Baptiste quietly asked Kate to join him in the hall. The nightmare really wasn't over yet. I gripped the blanket and wondered if Simone would press charges. Who could blame her if she did? *Reckless child endangerment, kidnapping?* Whether it was a misdemeanor or a felony, those charges were much worse than either joyriding or grand theft auto. I was petrified at the prospect.

I couldn't hear what was being said outside my door. The longer Kate was gone, the more apprehensive I became. At long last, the door opened and Kate came in, followed by Detective Baptiste. I sat up and searched their faces, they both looked pretty grim. My heart stopped. *This is it. I am going to prison for sure.*

Detective Baptiste came over and stood at the side of my bed. He looked at me for a long minute, took a deep breath, and said, "After careful consideration, Angel's mother has decided against pressing charges. This case is now closed . . . You are one lucky young lady, Miss April. I recommend you don't ever forget it."

He turned, nodded at Kate and they left the room.

Oh, thank God! I'm not going to prison!

I flopped back on the pillows, *Ouch!* My head still hurt. I'd been so terrified at the prospect of being incarcerated, I'd nearly forgotten about the concussion. I closed my eyes, said a little prayer of thanks to the universe for saving my butt, and fell into a deep, dreamless sleep.

When I awoke, it was morning again. The sun's golden rays streamed through the blinds and cast a halo around Kate, who was sitting patiently in the corner of my room.

"I brought your clothes. You're being released this morning," she said.

"Have you been here all night?"

"No. I came back about an hour ago. There was no point in staying the night, you were out of the woods." She pointed to the neatly folded clothes on the tray table. "Why don't you get dressed, so we can get out of here?"

"What about Angel? Is she all right? Is she going home, too?"

"Yes, Angel is going home today."

"Can I see her before we leave? I want to—no, I need to apologize to her and her mother."

"You get dressed, I'll go ask. You realize, they may not want to see you."

After Kate left, the nurse came in with a bag of prescriptions and instructions for me to take home.

Kate returned a few minutes later and shook her head. "Let's go home." Before pulling out of the parking garage, Kate turned towards me. "Breakfast or sleep?"

"Breakfast."

"Restaurant or home cooked?"

"Home cooked. You're a pretty good chef, you know."

"So I'm told."

I watched Kate smile for the first time in days. I, too, smiled for the first time in days. We drove back to the house through the

Quarter. I soaked up the sun, not at all bothered by the humidity. It was a Technicolor day; the sky an exceptional shade of blue, the pink and purple bougainvillea vibrant against the deep green of their vines. Everything felt fresh and new to me, as if I were seeing the city for the first time. Today, I had a much better understanding of what it meant when someone said you never fully appreciate something until you lose it.

I had come way too close to losing my freedom.

Chapter Twenty-Eight

Kate had chosen her car well; a Mini was exactly the right kind of car for zipping through the narrow French Quarter streets. She found a small space near the house and slipped the car right in. The house looked warm and inviting in the early morning sunlight. Kate unlocked the front door and we went inside. She left her keys and handbag on the beautiful marble-topped antique hall table and headed for the kitchen. I left the prescriptions on the table and followed.

"Please sit, I'll serve," she said, as she reached for a skillet hanging from the wrought iron pot rack.

"No, not this time, I'd like to help. What can I do?" I replied.

Kate arched an eyebrow in surprise. "Why don't you set the table?"

I took a small ceramic pot of fresh rosemary from the kitchen windowsill and centered it on the table. I tried to ignore the empty space where the antique mirror had hung over the sideboard, as I got out linen napkins and silver napkin rings from the drawer. I grabbed the jar of homemade strawberry jam and Kate's signature fleur-de-lis butter pats from the refrigerator and added them to my tablescape. I poured half-and-half into a delicate bone china pitcher, added matching coffee cups to the table, and got out the sugar bowl. I poured two glasses of orange juice.

I was admiring my handiwork when Kate said, "Breakfast is served." She slid the fluffy Denver omelets next to the perfectly crisped bacon and nicely browned toast and handed the plate to me.

Kate was right. There is something visceral about the food prep and the table prep and the satisfaction of a good meal. I couldn't help but smile. Maybe life did have a rewind button after all—sort of, anyway.

"*Bleat.*"

"BG! Oh my God! What are we going to do with BG? What'll happen to her?"

"Dunno, not really sure yet. I haven't had much time to think about BG. I might try making goat cheese, if she's able to produce milk. Or we might give her to a woman that I read about. She recently crowd-funded a local goat landscaping business and already has some city park contracts. She's hoping to expand the business. Until I work out a plan, BG will stay here with us."

I grew quiet and thought about the impending loss of my new four-legged friend.

"You know, April, goats are herd animals. BG is probably lonely for goat companionship . . . As much as I hate to admit it, it was an incredibly brave thing you did, not leaving BG behind to be sacrificed. She's pretty adorable. Believe it or not, it would have been perfectly legal for them to sacrifice her as part of their religious freedom."

"No way! Legal?"

"No matter how repugnant we find animal sacrifice to be, the right to do it was upheld at the Supreme Court level. There was an article in the paper a few years ago about a case in Florida. It addressed this very issue."

"Just because it's legal doesn't make it right, in my opinion, anyway. I wish I could have saved all of the chickens, too, but . . . well, you know, we were being chased and all," I said, avoiding Kate's gaze. "Aunt Kate?"

"Yes?"

"What did you and Detective Baptiste talk about outside my room at the hospital?"

"We talked about you specifically and teenagers in general. He's a cop and a father; he's had more than his fair share of encounters with teenaged foolhardiness. Some of the kids he told me about, well, let's just say they don't have the advantages that you do. You have opportunities ahead of you that they'll never have. Detective Baptiste offered to help in any way that he could to see that you get those opportunities. He also offered to let you sit in a jail cell for a few hours or maybe even overnight, to help you understand exactly what you avoided this time."

"Yikes! You didn't agree to that did you?"

"I did think about it. But no, I declined his generous offer."

"Um, did he say anything about Miles? Do you think I'll ever see him again?"

"I don't know what to tell you, April. You have some serious relationship repair that needs to be done with Miles and Angel and Simone. If they can be repaired at all."

"Uh, Aunt Kate, I'm not feeling well. I think I need some aspirin and some of that anti-itch stuff."

"I'll clean up the kitchen. You get into bed. The doctor said it would be a few more days before you fully recovered." Kate stacked the dishes, carried them to the sink. "F-Y-I, I've got both the afternoon and evening shifts today. I won't be back for dinner."

"You're leaving me alone?"

"I have no choice but to leave you alone. But you have a choice as to how you handle it," she replied.

There wasn't much I could say to that.

Kate crossed the room and stuck out her hand. "Let's start fresh, shall we?"

I took her outstretched hand, gave it a firm shake. "Yes, let's start this relationship over."

Totally depleted, I climbed the stairs to my room. I opened the door, looked into the sun-filled room, and was astounded to see that it had been "tossed." The armoire was wide open and had been emptied of all things Voodoo. The scarf, the books, the Voodoo doll, the anointing oil, the incense, and the candles lay strewn across my bed. Dresser drawers had been rummaged, but not closed; my clothes spilled over the edges. My computer had been turned on, my browser history reviewed and displayed for all to see. *Note to self: need a better password. Keep my browsing history cleared.*

The violation burned me; I wanted to confront Kate. At the top of the stairs I stopped to consider what it was I wanted to say. I was furious at the invasion of my privacy. I steamed towards the kitchen and was halfway there when it occurred to me that it was Detective Baptiste who had gone through my room. Or maybe he and Kate searched it when they were trying to piece together what had happened to me and to Kate's car and where I might be found, along with Angel, who had been reported missing. Only yesterday Kate pointed out I'd lost the right to complain about pretty much anything in my life. I turned around, crept back up the stairs, went into my room, closed the door, and got busy.

I straightened my clothes and pushed the drawers back into place. I couldn't get into bed without moving everything. I piled the candles, incense, anointing oil, and scarf on the dresser. I relocated Marguerite's books to the table by the chair, including the one I'd been reading a few nights ago, before my downward spiral into irrational behavior had started. Kate must have brought it back upstairs from the kitchen. I didn't need to decide anything now about what to do with everything that Marguerite had given me. My head ached. All I wanted was a hot shower, some of Kate's luscious lavender body powder, and more sleep.

And sleep I did, for hours. Around half past five, I awoke disoriented, drenched in sweat, desperately thirsty and with a pounding headache. The evening air was still, hot, thick with humidity, but I would manage. I slipped into a pair of shorts and a fresh tee shirt, then went into the bathroom and was freaked out by my own reflection. The scratches and bites were swollen and angry looking; I was a sore sight for eyes. I turned off the light and padded downstairs to get something cold to drink and something to eat. This time, there was no note from Kate hanging on the refrigerator. *Is this a sign that I'm home now, no longer just a visiting relative? Maybe, maybe not.* I helped myself to some food and a cold bottle of water, put everything on a tray, carried it out to the front porch, settled into one of the rocking chairs and watched the tourists stroll by. Tonight, I felt no need to join them.

"*Bleat!*"

Should I take BG for a walk? Probably not, it might be against some Louisiana law. I'd spent enough time with law enforcement in the past few days to last me a lifetime. Thinking about our tiny goat, I had a hard time understanding how animal sacrifice could not only exist in the twenty-first century, but be legal as well. It all seemed so . . . so *pagan*.

I watched a mule-drawn carriage, filled with laughing tourists swathed in colorful feather boas and gaudy strands of Mardi Gras beads, pass in front of the house. I flashed back to the carriage ride I'd had with Miles, remembered how delightful it had been. I hoped I hadn't completely screwed everything up with him. I missed Miles and his running commentary on New Orleans and his humor and his intelligence and, of course, his handsome face. I wondered if I should call him. I didn't have a cell phone any longer, but his number would be in my cloud account. Contacting him wouldn't be the problem. The problem was that it was probably too soon. I wondered if his father had played my statement for Miles, so he could hear what had happened. I wondered if Detective Baptiste had played the tape for Simone and she hadn't pressed charges because of my statement. I hoped that by now the tape had been played for everyone concerned. It would save me a lot of time, energy, and embarrassment trying to explain things.

All I wanted at this point was to simply move on to the apology portion of my life.

Chapter Twenty-Nine

After I finished my meal and tourist-watching, I cleaned up the dishes and settled in for some serious channel surfing. I flicked from channel to channel, but couldn't find anything on TV that held my interest. I turned the TV off and went outside to check on BG. She perked up when I opened the screen door. The courtyard was fully enclosed, with no way for her to escape. I assumed she was hooked up so she wouldn't chew on Kate's cushions, since goats had a bad rep for chewing on pretty much anything. I undid the tether and let her wander. She was so small, so adorable, so alone. Maybe it would be best for her to be with other goats, join a herd.

My thoughts turned to me and my circumstances. Dad was dead. Mom was God knew where in the Middle East, if she was even still alive. I had Kate, Angel, Simone, and Miles in my life, but my relationship with all of them was currently way less than stellar. I'd much rather Kate be my friend than my enemy. If I did as she asked, got a job and did her version of community service, it would probably help take care of mending her fence. Counseling? Ugh! I'd have to see if I could get out of it somehow. I had absolutely no interest in counseling. Baring my soul to a complete stranger was simply not going to happen if I could help it.

How would I ever get back in good graces with Angel and Simone? That would take some real planning. And Miles? He was a whole other story. He would take more time than planning.

As my all-time favorite heroine, Scarlett O'Hara, would say, "I'll think about it tomorrow . . . I'll think of some way to get him back. After all, tomorrow is another day!"

I watched BG nibble her way around the yard and was glad she was safe. If Angel and I hadn't been at the Voodoo ceremony, BG would be dead; I shuddered. Thinking back to the Voodoo ceremony, I was curious about the expression on Marguerite's face while I was escaping. She looked almost happy for me, which seemed strange. Perhaps, at that particular moment, I reminded her of her own daughter. I'd probably never know. Before he left the hospital, Detective Baptiste warned me again to stay away from Madame Marguerite and her Voodoo shop. I agreed it was for the best. What should I do with the Voodoo stuff? Throw it out? Box it up, mail it back to her? Keep everything as a reminder? Whatever, I'd figure it out later.

I hooked up BG for the evening and went inside to get fresh water for her. I wondered what goats ate besides grass; a bit of research on the Internet would help me find an answer. After booting up and perusing numerous websites, I discovered that goats like a variety of plants and weeds. Weeds in particular are high in nutrients for goats; that explained why goat landscaping businesses were popping up across the country. Eco-friendly weed clearing, how PC! It really would be the perfect place for BG to call home. For now, Kate's luxuriant courtyard was just fine. I was happy to have her here and would be sad to see her go.

I checked my e-mail. There was the usual spam and one e-mail from Sam. He had wired $750 to my account. Money was good. I needed a new phone and wasn't sure if the protection plan covered replacements. And I owed Kate money for the car detailing. He'd sent the rest of my things by ground; two trunks were scheduled to arrive soon. It would be good to have the rest of my things.

I looked around my mother's old room. It was quite a lovely, comfortable room, very bed-and-breakfast. For my taste, the room was a little too floral, a little too formal, most definitely not my style. I could easily make it mine with a few changes here and there. Switching out the current bedspread, chenille with little pink flowers cut into the design, for a plain white, lightweight quilted comforter would be a good start. *If it ever gets cool enough here to use a comforter, that is.* Something reversible would work: dark on one side, light on the other, like my ever-changing moods. My comfy chair was an absolute keeper. I looked down at the rug and spotted something peeking out from underneath the chair's pleated skirt. Curious, I went over to see what it was. I bent down and retrieved the photograph of Marie Laveau.

I curled up in the chair and studied the image of the enigmatic woman that had started it all, my great, great, great, great grandmother. *Who was this woman, really? How are we related? How exactly did our family happen?*

It was time to find out.

I removed *Women and New Orleans: A History* from the stack of books on the table and began to read, not in horror this time but with genuine interest. The chapter was titled "Marie Laveau, Voodoo Queen and Much More." The author described her as one of the most popular but least understood women in New Orleans history, a woman surrounded by myths. She was born sometime after 1790, and in 1827 had a daughter named Marie Laveau Paris. The daughter, who was one of fifteen children, carried on her mother's tradition of Voodoo rituals, curses, and cures. She passed away in 1890; her mother died in 1881.

There were only three pages of text. It didn't take long to finish reading, but now I was on fire, hungry for more. I wanted to know everything about this ordinary hairdresser who possessed an extraordinary gift for making people believe in her power. I wanted to know how she could be a practicing Catholic and a Voodoo high priestess at the same time. Most of all, I wanted to know where I fit in; Angel, too.

In a moment of clarity, I knew how I was going to repair my damaged relationship with Angel and Simone. I went back to my laptop, found the webpage for Ancestry.com, and got started. To begin with, I signed up for the free trial membership. I wasn't sure precisely how much information I would be able to add with the limited family history I knew of. I started a new tree and named it *April Claire Lockhart*. First, I added my personal details. Next, I added as much information as I could for my mother, my father, Kate, and my grandparents. While my focus for now was on the maternal side of the family, I was curious to know if there were any skeletons on my father's side of the family. At some point I would work on his branch, but not yet. I sat back and reviewed my efforts. It wasn't much, but it was a start. I was excited. I saved my tree, signed out of Ancestry.com, and got ready for bed.

My head was throbbing again. It was time to call it a night. I heard the front door open, then close. Kate was home from work. I thought it was best to give her some space. I needed space myself. The last few days had ground us both down; both of us were feeling pretty raw. I'd seen the tiredness in her face this morning and doubted it had gotten any better after a long day at the restaurant. I stayed in my room, shut off the lamp, and toddled to the bathroom using the glow from the laptop to light my way.

Before logging off the computer for the night, I typed in *Marie Laveau* and got over three hundred thousand web results. Research would take time but, at the moment, I had plenty of time. The doctor said I needed a few more days to recover. Not really enthusiastic about finding a job, I might milk the concussion thing a bit longer. After that, for sure I needed to find a job.

Having no real skills and ill-equipped to do much of anything, my job options were going to be limited to low-level drudge; I wasn't looking forward to it.

I could hardly wait to see what Kate had in mind for my community service. Most likely, more drudging. Whatever she had in mind, it would be seriously better than being incarcerated. Being behind bars was nobody's idea of a good time. I shut down the computer and climbed into bed.

Resting on the pillows, I inhaled the scent of night-blooming jasmine floating in on the warm summer breeze. I thought about Miles. The best thing to happen to me in a long time was meeting Miles and I'd completely blown it.

What kind of crazy am I? How on earth am I ever going to redeem myself? Will I even be able to?

Chapter Thirty

I awoke to yet another morning of blazing sunlight streaming through the window. Unquestionably, it was time to consider a room-darkening shade. I'd never been an early riser and wasn't inclined to start now. Once again, the air was filled with delicious aromas wafting up from downstairs. I threw back the sheet, got out of bed and padded to the bathroom. Eek! Ugh! My face was still a bumpy red mess; arms and legs, too, though not as bad as yesterday. I slathered on the antibiotic ointment, carefully dressed in shorts, tank top, and slippers, and headed for the kitchen.

"Morning," said Kate.

"Morning," I said, pouring myself a glass of orange juice.

I sat at the table, which hadn't been set for breakfast. Another sign I was no longer a guest here?

"What are you making now? Whatever it is, it smells really good."

"Since you're grounded and you won't be going out in public until your wounds heal and your concussion is gone, I wanted to have a variety of healthy food choices in the house. I've grilled some vegetables and am roasting a turkey breast. There are homemade veggie burgers in the freezer and pretzel rolls in the bread bin. Would you like the vegetables plain or marinated with a little lemon juice and olive oil?"

"I'm good either way, whatever is easiest for you," I replied. "Thank you for doing this."

Kate got a juicer from under the counter, retrieved a bottle of extra-virgin olive oil from the pantry, and took two fresh lemons from a wire basket near the window. She squeezed the lemon juice, added a pinch each of salt and pepper to the olive oil, and whisked everything together. She sprinkled the citrus vinaigrette over the vegetables; the whole process had taken her less than ten minutes. Really impressive.

"*Bleat!*"

"How's BG this morning?" I asked.

"She's fine. I don't know anything about goats, but she looks pretty happy here. She likes my grass, I guess."

"Have you decided yet what we're going to do with her?"

"I haven't. I'd like to find out at what point she can give milk. I wouldn't mind trying my hand at making fresh cheese. I need to find out if I can even keep a farm animal in the city. The answers to those questions will help me decide a course of action. You're quite fond of her, aren't you?"

"Well, yeah! Extreme circumstances create extreme bonds, right? Would you like me to find out for you about the milk thing? I bet I can find the answer on the Internet. I can try researching city regulations for farm animals, too, if you'd like."

I rambled on and told Kate everything I had learned about goat diets the night before.

Kate looked at me and smiled, "Yes, I'd very much like for you to help. You're pretty good with computers? Like your dad?"

"I guess so. I think I learned quite a bit from him, more than I realized. I'm not anywhere near as good as he was, though. But, then again I.T. was his profession."

"I'm sorry I never really got to know him. He sounds like he was a good father."

"He was. You would have liked him."

"I did like him. Very much. He was always nice to me when he came over to see Julia. That was such a long time ago. I haven't seen him since your mom got pregnant. Not surprisingly, he was banned from coming around here."

I traded my empty juice glass for a mug filled with steaming hot coffee and a little cream. I selected a muffin from under the glass dome and sat back down at the table.

"Did your mother teach you how to cook?"

Kate laughed, "Good heavens, no. I know it sounds like an old joke, but the only thing she ever made was a reservation. I learned from our cook, Sadie Lee. Her biscuits were so light that if you didn't get them covered in her pan gravy right away, they'd float right off your plate! Sadie Lee instilled in me a passion for food. We'd cook and laugh for hours on end. It was the best part of my childhood. Growing up, I devoured cookbooks like they were romance novels. I spent most of my free time learning from Sadie Lee; learning things that were never written in cookbooks, tricks of the trade so to speak. I always knew I'd be a chef."

Kate continued, "What about you, April? What do you want to do with your life? What's your passion?"

"Um . . . I don't know. I don't think I have a passion for anything. I've never really thought about it."

"Well, you're still young. You have time to decide. In the meantime, you can try different things, see what fits. And that brings me to this." Kate reached into her carry-all, retrieved the morning paper, and handed it to me.

"Here you go. You can start looking through today's classified ads to get an idea of what jobs are available. I left a map of the French Quarter for you on the hall table. It's time you learned your way around."

Yikes, that was fast, I didn't think I'd have to start looking so soon.
"Kate?"

"Yes?"

"I'm happy to look at today's paper, but would it be all right if I set up interviews for a few days from now, or maybe next week, after my face heals up? I don't want to scare anybody off."

"Not a problem. Go through the ads, circle the ones you think you might be interested in. Look at the map, find out where they're located, call them up and see what you can do. Once you find a job and get a schedule, we'll sort out your community service and get you set up for counseling."

"I *don't* need therapy." I pouted and pushed my chair away from the table, ready to bolt.

"Since you won't talk to me about your parents, grief counseling is on your horizon. You don't have a choice."

When the timer sounded, she turned away from me to remove the turkey from the oven. Kate, looking very much like the star of a Thanksgiving commercial, turned back around and presented a crispy golden brown turkey breast. She inserted a meat thermometer and, satisfied it was done, covered the fragrant breast with a tin foil tent, leaving it to rest on the counter. She chopped up some flat-leaf parsley and sprinkled the bits over the grilled, marinating vegetables, then stretched plastic wrap over the platter and put it in the refrigerator. Her movements were effortless, practiced. Watching her was like having a private showing from a Food Network celebrity. I was in awe of her expertise, or at least I would have been if I hadn't been so annoyed about the grief counseling thing.

"I never asked, April, but what kind of food do you like? Do you have preferences? Food allergies? Anything you could tell me would be helpful. If you'd like anything in particular from the market, make a list and put it on the refrigerator door. I'll pick it up for you," said Kate, her cheerfulness sounding a bit forced.

"Thank you."

"My apologies, but I'll be out of the house most of the day today. I had hoped to spend some quality time with you this morning, but my schedule got jammed up. Later in the week, perhaps?"

"No problem. I have things to do anyway," I said, waving my newspaper. "Whatever I find out about goats and milk production, I'll print out for you. I'll leave everything on your desk, same for any farm animal regulations. If I feel well enough, I'll get back on your photo-scanning project. Have you thought about Photoshop?"

"It's on my list of things to do today. Do you know how to install it?"

I rolled my eyes. "Yes, I know how to install it. Not a problem."

"Thank you for taking care of this project for me. I've wanted to scan those photographs for a long time," she said.

Our conversation had turned excessively formal and claustrophobic. I needed to get out of the kitchen.

"May I be excused?"

"Yes, of course. You can go," said Kate, who seemed as anxious for me to go as I was ready to leave.

I cleared the table, put my mug in the dishwasher, picked up the newspaper, said "goodbye" and "have a lovely day" to Kate, and left the kitchen.

I collected the map from the hall table and went back to my room, closing the door a little harder than I needed to. I slouched in my comfy chair and kicked off my slippers. My bedroom was rapidly becoming my "go to" place, my safe haven. I wanted to throw the newspaper, but didn't. Instead I set it and the map on top of the stack of books. I had no choice, I needed to find a job soon—but I didn't need to search for one right this minute. Kate would be gone most of the day. I had loads of time and could spend it any way I wanted, as long as it was within the confines of this house.

I had no ankle monitor, but clearly I was under house arrest.

Chapter Thirty-One

It was only 7:30, way too early for me. I looked around the room. *Where should I begin?* First things first: I got up, retrieved the bag Marguerite had given me, cleared the dresser of all Voodoo swag, and put everything back in the armoire. Final destination TBD.

I looked at the clock, 7:35. A whole five minutes had elapsed. My day was going well so far. I sat in the chair and looked around the room again, but couldn't find my focus. I felt restless, caged. I wanted Kate to leave, to get on with her day, so I could get on with mine. I wanted to start my research on Marie Laveau. I was already alone in my room, but I wanted to be alone in the house. I didn't want to be interrupted once I delved deeper.

I picked up the map, flipped it open then over. It was a colorful laminated double-sided thing with indexes for streets, government buildings, hospitals, and points of interest. I found our block on Royal between Ursulines and Governor Nicholls. I traced my finger from our place to Royal and Marigny, where Miles lived with his dad. It wasn't very far. I traced my finger in the opposite direction on Royal and found the police station where Detective Baptiste worked. Over by the Mississippi River, was Café du Monde, where Miles had taken me for beignets and café au lait. The French Quarter was laid out in a simple grid pattern; I now understood why it was so easy to get around. Everything was within walking distance.

I picked up the newspaper. The headlines were of no interest. The weather was of no interest. Big shock—it was going to be hot and humid today, just like every other day in New Orleans. The classifieds were of no interest, but I had no choice. I needed to get started with my job search and get it out of the way. When Kate got home tonight, she would ask me to report on my efforts. Kate was very old-school, she apparently didn't know anything about searching for jobs online. Since I wasn't overly enthusiastic at the prospect of getting a job in the first place, especially a low-level one, I saw no point in speeding up the process by telling her about how user-friendly the job-hunting search engines are.

There were loads of ads for waitresses. Since I was under the age of eighteen, I couldn't serve alcohol and what's a meal in New Orleans without alcohol? Breakfast?

Moving on. *Oh, boy! They're looking for baggers at the grocery store. I'll pass on that opportunity.* Okay, here's an ad for a food presenter in a gourmet market; this could be a candidate. I wasn't exactly sure what a food presenter did, but doubted it was a highly skilled profession. In my current condition, gourmet food presentation might not be all that appetizing to customers, but I circled it in red anyway and continued to read.

Okay, here's a position that's sort of mind-boggling: a research company is looking for smokers, ten years to sixteen years old, who want to stop. *Even if I did smoke, I'm too old for this gig! How crazy is that?*

Finding any job, much less something I wanted or could do, was going to be much harder than I thought. What a pain in the neck, or lower. My thoughts twisted in a truly bizarre direction. After all I'd been through lately, I could probably get a job at the Voodoo shop with Marguerite. I certainly had practical experience now, right? I immediately squashed the thought and dragged it to my mental recycle bin.

Kate rapped on my door and said, "Goodbye. Enjoy your day." I called out, "Back at ya! See you later!"

I heard the front door open, then close. I was finally alone. I set the newspaper aside and decided to do the goat research, get it ready for Kate and check it off my "to do" list. I sat on the bed, propped up the laptop, and booted up. Not knowing how to research the law, I typed in my question: *Is it legal to keep a goat within the New Orleans city limits* and clicked on the Search button. I didn't find much to start with. However, I did learn there is a distinction between "companion animals" and "livestock." I began to search deeper.

I was on the verge of giving up when I located a document that looked like it might hold an answer for Kate: *Louisiana Revised Statutes. Title 9. Civil Code Ancillaries.* It addressed the *Limitation of Liability of Farm Animal Activity.* I scanned through a section called *Statute Text.* After reading through the legal language, I determined BG didn't fit the category of Farm Animal, or that making goat cheese would be considered Farm Animal Activity. BG was just one little goat, more pet than productive.

I sent the document to the printer and started my search for information on milking goats. I poked around on the Internet some more and learned quite a bit about milk goats. However, without knowing what breed of goat BG was, it was kind of a waste of my time. We would need to consult with a goat professional, either the landscaper or a vet. I printed out the information for the goat landscaper and a list of local vets.

I organized the morning's work product and left everything on Kate's desk. Her desk clock chimed the hour. I'd been totally engrossed at the computer for hours. I was pleased with my progress. At last, I'd found something I was good at: research. I loved it! I especially liked reading the legal documents. Even though I didn't understand all of it, I understood enough. My grandfather and great-grandfather on my mother's side had been lawyers. *Is the law in my DNA? It would be so much more socially acceptable than my genetic connection to Voodoo, right?*

I was stiff, headachy, and hungry. It was time for my afternoon break. Lunch outside appealed to me. I decided to make a salad for BG. I padded down to the kitchen, opened the fridge, and removed the salad ingredients. I shredded lettuce and carrots for her and prepared a plate of grilled vegetables, cheese, and a home-made pretzel roll for myself. I filled a glass with tea, got a cold bottle of water for BG, loaded everything onto a tray and carried it outside. I released BG from her tether, set down her bowl of salad and refilled her water dish from the chilled bottle.

"*Bleat!*" A goat thank-you to me before she began grazing, I assumed.

BG wasn't a fast eater, but it didn't take long before the dish was empty and she began to wander, nibbling here and there around the courtyard. *What a sweetie! How cool would it be if we kept her?*

I sat at the wrought iron table, savoring every morsel of marinated vegetables and thinking about how to go about my research of Marie Laveau this afternoon. *Where's the best place to start? Just type in* Marie Laveau *and little by little, narrow my search? Ancestry.com might have something useful. Maybe there's already a Laveau family tree set up and whoever created the tree was missing our family information?* I didn't know much about Ancestry.com except what I learned from their TV commercials and the little bit of work I did setting up my own tree last night.

I definitely needed more information about Kate, Mom, and my grandmother. *Does Kate have copies of their birth certificates in the files in her office?* I wondered if Angel's mother's last name was her maiden name or her married name. For that matter, I didn't know if she was ever married. I made a mental note to do an Internet search to check if there was anything out in cyberspace about Simone. It was doubtful she had a social media presence, but you could never tell what you might find that other people had posted without your knowledge or consent. That was a frightening thought. *Note to self: do a search of my own name, see what pops up.*

I sopped up the last of the vinaigrette with the last bit of pretzel roll and washed it down with the last of the tea. I'd enjoyed yet another meal filled with incredibly delicious food from Kate's kitchen. This was getting to be a habit, and not a bad one either. I considered bringing BG inside to keep me company, but didn't want to push my already tenuous luck if Kate came back home early. I tethered BG, cleared the table, and went back inside. After putting the dishes in the dishwasher and putting the tray away, I poured myself a refill of tea and filled a clean plate from the cabinet with cookies from the glass jar on the sideboard. Growing up, I hardly ever ate desserts. Now I couldn't get enough of Kate's daily homemade sweets. Stress will do that to a person. This morning she'd baked some sort of crunchy cinnamon cookies with pecans, reminiscent of Simone's Angel Crunch Cookies. It made me sad to think back on that morning at Angel's house, just a few days earlier.

Fortified now, my headache gone, I was ready to get back at it. Upstairs, I once again got comfortable on the bed, logged back in, and started digging with my cyber shovel.

Chapter Thirty-Two

Uncertain where to begin, I started with the two most basic questions: what is Voodoo and who was Marie Laveau? I typed in *definition of Voodoo*, hit Search, and found that there were over three million available results that defined Voodoo, in addition to the over three hundred thousand Marie Laveau websites. I needed to understand what Voodoo was before I could understand who Marie Laveau was, so I started with a dictionary. The Oxford Dictionary website defined Voodoo as:

A black religious cult practiced in the Caribbean and the southern US, combining elements of Roman Catholic ritual with traditional African magical and religious rites, and characterized by sorcery and spirit possession.

The Simple English Wikipedia website expounded on the subject:

In Voodoo many gods and spirits are prayed to or called on. Both spirits of nature and of dead people are important. The spirits of family member who have died are especially important. Voodoo often has rituals with music and dancing. Drums are used to make most of this music. In Voodoo people often believe that a spirit is in their body and controlling the body. Having a spirit come into is wanted, and important. This spirit can speak for the gods or dead people you love, and can also help to heal or do magic.

I flashed back to my time with Marguerite in the swamp and recoiled at the memory. I shook the feeling off and moved on. I started my search of Marie Laveau. I began to read what looked to be the more substantive, less sensational websites dedicated to her. I spent hours scanning through information. Anything I thought might be relevant was printed out. Whether or not it would be useful to me, or even accurate, was yet to be determined.

I learned Marie Catherine Laveau was born a free woman of color in New Orleans on or about September 10, 1801; the actual date was unconfirmed. A child of biracial parents, she was baptized in St. Louis Cathedral by Père Antoine, who later became her close friend and confidant. At the age of seventeen, Marie married a Haitian refugee, a carpenter named Jacques Paris. They had a daughter (some sources said two daughters), who apparently died not long after Jacques Paris disappeared in the early 1820s. After he'd been missing for one full year, Jacques Paris was declared dead and Marie began calling herself the "Widow Paris." It was rumored, but never proved, that she was involved in "disappearing" her husband to escape an unhappy marriage.

There were also claims that Marie had an illegitimate daughter, Delphine, with an unnamed white man, and that Marie later gave her up to be raised by a "white" family. It was also reported that Delphine gave birth to a very dark skinned daughter, Liga, who she gave to her mother, Marie Laveau, to raise as her own child. Delphine told her husband their baby had been stillborn, which was a fairly common occurrence in those days. I hadn't found any documentation that validated this information; so far, it was all supposition. It didn't mean the information wasn't out there floating somewhere in cyberspace; I just hadn't found it yet. I needed to dig deeper.

Reported to be stunningly beautiful, Marie Laveau attracted the eye of Jean Louis Christophe Duminy de Glapion, the eldest son of a wealthy Louisiana sugar plantation owner. As interracial marriages were illegal in Louisiana, Marie couldn't marry her white lover. They coexisted in a common-law relationship for nearly thirty years. Some websites indicated they produced as many as fifteen children, some said only seven; again, I had found no verifiable documentation. One source confirmed five children, three of whom were daughters, all of whom were named Marie, as was the custom at the time. Of the five apparently documented children, only two daughters survived to adulthood; one of them became her mother's successor in the practice of Voodoo.

Well, darn, this was going to be considerably more difficult than I'd originally thought. How could I find out anything about children that were never documented? Where would I go for that kind of information if I couldn't find it on the Internet? A library? Church records? City archives? There's gotta be New Orleans research centers listed on the Internet. I'll start there. I might actually have to go old-school and pull hard-copy records myself.

I kept digging, but found little that made sense to me regarding her children. I switched gears. I wanted to understand how Marie Laveau could be a practicing Catholic, could attend Mass on Sunday mornings and hold Voodoo ceremonies in the evenings. Maybe like the dictionary said, it was because the two religions had certain elements in common. What I was most curious about was how she became involved in Voodoo in the first place. The more I learned about her, the more questions I had.

I reached for another cookie, but the plate was empty, the iced tea glass drained. I looked out the window and realized it was already dusk. It wouldn't be much longer before Kate would be home. I got up from the bed and worked out the kinks—stretching my arms to the ceiling, bending down and touching my toes, shaking out my arms. I'd been sitting way too long. Down to the kitchen to put my dishes in the dishwasher, grab some water, and go outside. I released BG from her tether and watched as she wandered around the courtyard, a nibble here, a nibble there.

I sat at the wrought iron table and reviewed what I had learned so far. Marie Laveau had a white grandfather and an African grandmother. Her parents were mixed-race. She was the widow of a Haitian carpenter and the common-law wife of a white sugar plantation heir. She had an unconfirmed number of children. Marie Laveau could neither read nor write, but apparently was able to accomplish much within New Orleans society without a formal education. She was a respected businesswoman. She was a talented hairdresser. She was a skilled nurse. She owned property. She also had the ear of local politicians and priests. As described in everything I'd read so far this afternoon, she had a captivating personality. I found her more than intriguing.

My thoughts shifted elsewhere. I reflected on one piece of history that I found especially personal and deeply disturbing. It was a common practice in the 1800s for mothers who gave birth to mixed-race children, with either predominately white or black skin tones, to give up their children to be raised by a family consistent with the color of their skin. *Would mothers give up their babies because it was in the best interest of the child, or were they simply motivated by self-interest?* There was absolutely no way to tell what would motivate any mother to abandon her child. I could sort of understand the need for such family "adjustments" in the 1800s, when racism ruled. *Why did my mother abandon me? What was her excuse? Why didn't she fight for me?*

Returning from my dark reverie, I shifted my focus again. I considered everything I had learned so far about Marie Laveau's mixed-race heritage and her relationships with both black and white men and the reports of up to fifteen mixed-race children. It was a lot of information to process. When I included the photographs in Angel's house and Kate's office in my analysis, everything seemed to support my theory that Simone, Angel, Kate, and I were related. My next step would be to authenticate everything to the best of my ability and then share it with my new family.

It was getting late; time to get back to work. I got up and corralled BG, kissing her little head and giving her a few ear snuggles before hooking her back up for the evening. I checked her water bowl and went back inside. I opened the refrigerator and was staring at the contents, trying to decide about dinner, when I heard the front door open, then close. Kate was home. I shut the refrigerator door and leaned against the counter, waiting for her to come into the kitchen. Hopefully, she would make the dinner decision for us.

"Hey, welcome home! I was just thinking about you, wondering what you might like for dinner."

"Glad to be home. I'm beyond pooped," said Kate, as she set down her tote bag and kicked off her clogs. "How about we order a pizza? I don't feel like cooking tonight. I doubt you're ready to go out in public yet with your face looking like that, even though it looks like you're healing pretty quickly. You'll be ready for public appearances fairly soon."

"Pizza's great! Can we do veggie? We could do half and half, if you'd like sausage or pepperoni."

"I pretty much eat everything. Veggie is fine with me. Thick or thin crust? I'll place the order and go shower. You can tell me about your day over dinner."

"Thin crust. Can we get salad too, Italian dressing on the side? I'll set the table while you freshen up. What would you like to drink?"

"This'll do for me," said Kate, removing a bottle of red wine from the rack on the counter. She opened it, sniffed the cork and poured a glass.

"I should probably let this breathe, but, oh, well, not tonight." Kate raised her glass to me. "Cheers!" She placed the order, topped off her glass of wine, and headed to the shower.

"Well, okay, then! A soda will do for me," I said to Kate's back.

I got out plates, salad bowls, and napkins and began to set the table. After adding jars of crushed red pepper, oregano, grated Parmesan, and the bottle of wine to the table, I slid the napkins into their rings, centered them on the plates and straightened the forks and knives. Something was missing. I took an ornate silver candlestick with an ivory-colored beeswax taper from the butler's pantry and placed it with matches from the "catch-all drawer" in the center of the table between our plates.

Surveying the table, I was pleased. *I'm getting pretty good at this table setting thing. Besides, it won't hurt my case any if I do something nice for Kate. It's worth a shot anyway. I hope when she comes downstairs, she'll be nice and relaxed, maybe even a little buzzed from the wine and, hopefully, too tired to get involved in heavy conversation.* I could help move her in that direction. I poured a fresh glass of wine and set it down next to Kate's plate. *That should do it.*

It wasn't long before Kate was back in the kitchen, her skin a bright pink, as if she had tried to scrub the day off.

"Bad day?" I asked.

"Not bad, just hectic. We had a full house, were short-staffed and turned every table two or three times. After lunch, we began the prep for a private event this evening, which, mercifully, I'm not working." Kate nodded her head towards the table. "Nice job on the table. Thanks for the fresh glass of wine, it was very insightful of you," she said, draining the last of the first glass and putting it in the sink.

The doorbell chimed and Kate left to pay the delivery person. I chose a wine glass for myself, filled it with ice, popped the soda can and set them at my place. I was lighting the candle when Kate came back with the food.

"Nice touch. Let's eat!"

Chapter Thirty-Three

"Good pizza," I said, sliding another piece onto my plate.

"It is, isn't it? It's from my favorite pizza place. When the business first started, the owners only sold pizza by the slice out of a hole-in-the-wall place in the French Quarter. Slice by slice, they grew a loyal following, especially with the filmmakers who came down here to make their movies. Today, it's a full-service restaurant." said Kate.

"Nice! Can I ask you something?"

"Sure."

"Where do chefs go to eat? Do you go check out the competition, the latest and greatest new chefs?"

"Indeed I do! We all do it. We all know each other, if not personally, at least by reputation. It's a relatively small trendy restaurant community and the trendier the restaurant is, the harder it is to stay in business. It's good to see what's working and what isn't. There aren't that many new, too-chic-for-words establishments, but there are quite a few well-established, historic restaurants like Galatoire's and Antoine's or any one of the numerous Brennan family restaurants."

She continued, "The locals aren't really big on change, everyone has their favorites. Of course the tourists expect the famous centuries-old standbys to be here when they come to town. They want to be able to tell the folks back home all about where and what they ate while visiting New Orleans," said Kate, washing down the last bite of pizza with a little more wine.

"Where do you like to go? Like if you're on a date or something?" I asked.

"It depends on the date. Sometimes, say for a casual movie date, a couple of Lucky Dogs on the way and some popcorn at the theater will suffice. Maybe a quick stop at the Red Fish Grill or the Acme Oyster House for a plate of oysters afterwards. For something a little more romantic, there are quite a few restaurants with exquisite courtyards and, for the most part, they are all walking distance from here," said Kate, yawning deeply.

"More wine?" I asked, holding the bottle up, ready to pour.

Kate tipped her empty glass towards me, then looked at the half-empty bottle and said, "No thanks. I've had enough, I should keep my wits about me."

"Why?"

"Why, what?"

"Why do you need to keep your wits about you? Why do you always need to be in control? Don't you ever loosen up?"

Kate hesitated, narrowed her eyes, frosted her tone, and said, "Those are all very good questions, April. None are any of your business. Well, on second thought, maybe one question is your business. *I* need to keep my wits about me because *I* don't know what crazy-assed thing *you'll* do next."

Ooops! Just when things were going so well. She was relaxed and distracted, then Boom, I blew it.

I put the bottle down, lowered my eyes, and said, "Point taken." I began to stack the dishes and hoped that was the end of it, but knew it wouldn't be.

"So, April, now that you've effectively killed my buzz and any hope of nodding off to dreamland in the next twenty minutes, let's talk about you and your day. Tell me about your job search. How did it go? Did you find anything yet?"

Well, here we go, exactly what I was trying to avoid: heavy conversation. I just can't get out of my own way, no matter what I do. Unbelievable. I finished stacking the dishes, rinsed them in the sink, and loaded them into the dishwasher.

I got the cork from the counter, took it over to the bottle, and asked once more, "Are you sure?"

"I'm sure."

I corked the bottle and sat back down at the table.

"I did as you asked. I read through every ad for part-time jobs. I found one that might work out and circled it so we could talk about it. I left the newspaper on your desk, should I go get it?" I asked, rising to escape.

"Not now."

I settled back into my chair. "I'll look again tomorrow after the paper gets here. I don't have any job experience, so it's kinda hard."

I told her about the different job openings listed in the classifieds. She laughed at some of them, but, like me, was horrified by the ad for the smokers aged ten to sixteen.

"Okay. Anything else to report?" she asked.

"Yeah! I found a bunch of stuff on goats as pets—excuse me, *companion animals.* I printed out what I thought you might think was pertinent, organized it, and left the information on your desk. I also found a law I believe answers a lot of the questions we had about keeping goats as pets. Last thing, I left you the phone numbers for the landscaping company and the local vets who have goat patients."

Kate said, "Thank you for that. I've been thinking about BG. Even though I think a goat would be a charming and interesting pet, one that would suit you to a "T" since you're as stubborn as one, I came to the conclusion she'd still be better off with other goats. She can stay here until I can get her settled elsewhere. I'll call the landscaper tomorrow to see what I can work out."

"I suppose you're right. She looks sort of lonesome out there in your courtyard." Hoping to plant a seed, I added, "Did you know that people who have pygmy goats as pets let them sleep indoors on their beds like dogs? Isn't that amazing?"

"Amazing, yes, but not going to happen here. She goes as soon as I find the right place for her. Maybe you can visit. Or better yet, maybe you can get a job with the landscaping company. It can't take too much training to be a goat herder."

My face fell as hard as a fifty-pound weight dropped from a fifty-foot height.

Kate laughed, "What's wrong? Did I get your goat?"

"Not funny!"

"Anything else?" she asked.

"No, not really. I rested like the doctor recommended. I napped, surfed the Net for a while, spent time with BG, nothing much else. One thing I did learn today was how much I liked research."

I was excited, but stopped talking before I revealed more than I had intended. I wasn't ready to talk about Marie Laveau yet.

"Research?" asked Kate. "What kind of research?"

Oh boy. Think, April, think!

"Well, um, the research I did on the goats, of course. I really got into it and spent hours reading the different sites. It's kind of addictive. I especially liked finding the different laws, the *statutes*, I mean."

"Well now, that is interesting. Maybe you inherited something besides your independence from our side of the family. I still keep in touch with the man that bought Dad's law firm. I could reach out to him if you'd like. An internship might work for you."

"I'll think about it." I squirmed in my chair like a two-year-old. I was beyond ready to call it a night.

Kate looked at me, "We still have a few more things to talk about—grief counseling, community service, and school."

"School?"

"Yes, school. It's the end of June already. School starts middle to end of August. I need to get you registered somewhere soon. I want you to give some thought about where you would like to go. Your mother and I attended a Catholic all-girls school, but you can go to a public school if you like. I'll check around to see who recommends what. I'll call Sam tomorrow so he can get your transcripts organized. We're going to need them."

Ugh, I'd forgotten all about school. This day was so not ending well.

"Okay, I'll give it some thought."

"Now, grief counseling. I'm going to table that until you're healed up and able to comfortably go out in public. I anticipate your first session will be in about a week, ten days at the most from the way your scratches and bites look."

I bristled at the thought. "Really? Grief counseling? I'm perfectly fine, I don't need anybody. I mean, I don't need to talk to anybody, especially a stranger."

"No doubt we have a difference of opinion on the subject. You need to talk to someone about what's happened. If you aren't going to open up to me, your only alternative is to open up to a stranger. It's your call."

"Whatever." I wrapped my arms tightly around my chest, slid farther down in the chair. My foot tapped wildly. I was anxious to get this unbearable evening over with.

"I saved the best for last."

"Do tell," I growled.

"Community service. I've chosen something for you, which, in my humble opinion, will benefit you much more than picking up road trash with a spiked pole, like prison trustees do."

"What?" I sat up straight, ready to bolt.

"New Orleans has a few facilities where 'at-risk' teens are taught culinary skills. They get equipped to go out into the world and make a way for themselves. You, my dear, are going to volunteer some of your time with them. I've already started making arrangements for you."

"Seriously? What on earth do I have to offer them? I can't teach them anything. I don't know anything!"

I was on total overload, on the verge of tears.

Kate replied softly, "April, honey, this isn't about what you can teach *them*. This is about what they can teach *you*."

Chapter Thirty-Four

Kate stood, cleared the rest of the table, and said, "Let's call it a night."

She didn't have to tell me twice. I pushed back from the table. "Thanks for dinner. Goodnight."

I fled the room. I heard the back door open and knew she was checking on BG one last time before turning in. Back in the safety of my room, I threw myself on the bed and pounded my fists like a child at the height of the "terrible twos." I felt trapped and alone, and I had accomplished this all by myself. I ached to call Miles. I wanted to hear those soothing Southern tones telling me everything would be all right. I missed my friend terribly and feared I would never be able to make things right again. Sorrow ruled the rest of my evening until I crashed, still face down on the bed.

I awoke the following morning soaked with sweat and with my face buried in the pillow. Gazing at my reflection in the bathroom mirror, I was horrified by the number of pillow wrinkles creasing the ugly scratches and bites; my face looked like a roadmap to Hell. I was a mess, inside and out. I ran the tap until the water was icy cold, then soaked a washcloth and held it to my face. I wasn't sure it would help, but it certainly felt good. After a five-minute shower, I opened the tube of antibiotic ointment and covered the scratches. I wound my damp curls into a knot, got dressed, and headed to the kitchen. The newspaper was lying on the kitchen table, opened and folded at the classified ads for part-time jobs. *How thoughtful . . . not.*

Another note was under the magnet on the fridge:

Gone for the day, see you tonight. Here are the names of two schools. Please look them up on the Internet, see what you think. We'll talk about it tonight. Kate. PS, Here is the name of the facility where you'll be volunteering your time. Check out their website and get familiar. One last thing, please try to make some progress with my scanning project. K. PPS, Stay out of trouble.

I crumpled up the note, aimed for the trash and made the basket. *Score one for me.* I poured a glass of juice, sliced an apple, and went outside to have breakfast.

"*Bleat!*"

"Good morning to the sweetest little goat in the whole wide world!" I sat down beside her, gave her an ear snuggle.

"BG, you are the only good thing to come out of my ill-conceived Voodoo escapade. I'll be truly sorry to see you go. You're the only one I can talk to who doesn't criticize or judge or tell me what to do. You simply listen to me."

"*Bleat!*"

"Want some apple?"

"*Bleat!*"

BG took the slice and began to crunch; I did the same. I thought about the day ahead.

Little by little, I began to put things in perspective. I was cheered by the fact I wasn't in county lockup. That was a very good thing, no question. I was under modified house arrest by Kate, but all in all, at the end of the day, I was pretty darned lucky to have dodged the jail-time bullet. Once again, I said a little prayer of thanks to the universe.

"Okay, BG, let us review, shall we?

"Number one, school. I need to finish high school anyway, so really, it's no big deal to look into the options available. At least Kate's giving me a choice in this. Could be worse.

"Number two, community service. Well, yeah, I hated the thought of it, but it wouldn't kill me. Better to do it now, just get it over with and try to redeem myself with everyone, especially Miles. I need him to understand I'm not some maniac who went completely off the rails. I'd only taken a bit of a side trip.

"Number three, job. T-B-D.

"Number four, grief counseling. I need to work out some sort of reasonable angle to get Kate to let that slide. Need a plan.

"Number five, photo scanning. Kate's project is definitely doable, no problem. It could be interesting, probably necessary for creating my ancestry tree.

"Number six, family tree. A little more difficult than originally thought, but still doable. I may need to enlist Kate and Simone to provide some family history to fill in the gaps. I could definitely work that to my advantage; maybe help bring us all together, which is my ultimate goal.

"This all makes sense to you, right, BG?"

"*Bleat!*"

I finished my breakfast and left fresh water for BG. Back inside, I got the newspaper and a bottle of water and headed upstairs to start my day. My room was, like every other day, stifling, so I moved my laptop and other stuff out to the balcony off Kate's office and flipped the switch for the outdoor ceiling fan. Among my e-mails was the usual junk and one from Sam, a cc: to me in response to Kate's request for transcripts. He would handle everything and get the records to her ASAP.

Next, I pulled up the website for my cell carrier, looked at new phones, found a nice replacement for the one I lost in the swamp, ordered it, and checked it off my mental list of things to do. I'd have a new, no-cost phone by the end of the week. I closed the web page, sat back and gave a moment of silent appreciation to Dad for insisting on loss insurance when he bought the phone for me. That was so typical of him, always looking out for me.

I perused the paper; nothing much that was new had been added to the classifieds since yesterday. I only needed one job that was the right fit for me. Halfway down the page, I found it! Café Beignet was looking for a counter person/server. That was the place where I bought the cemetery tour ticket and met Miles; it seemed like forever ago now. They didn't need someone with experience; the ad said they were willing to train "an enthusiastic, energetic, entrepreneur-type person." *This sounds like me, right? And it puts me in close proximity to Miles almost daily! If I have any Voodoo magic in my DNA at all, I would do my best to work it on him. I needed my friend back.*

I ran into Kate's office and dialed the number, hoping I could set up an interview soon, but not before I could buy some heavy-duty makeup to hide the ugly scratches. The manager answered on the third ring. She said I was the first person to respond to the ad and she appreciated such enthusiasm so early in the morning. By the end of the call, we were both laughing and I was scheduled to meet with her in person the following afternoon. I would be her first interview and, hopefully, the last. I was determined to snag the job.

I looked at the boxes of photographs on the office floor but decided to leave them for later. What I wanted to do now was go read up on potential high schools for my senior year and get that out of the way. The first school on Kate's list was a charter school that had forty teachers, eight hundred students, and a student-teacher ratio of 20:1. The student body was 60 percent male, 40 percent female. Advanced Placement participation was at 93 percent and the college readiness index was at 82.6 percent. It listed an enrollment of 54 percent minorities and 28 percent economically disadvantaged. Sounded like a good possibility for me.

Next up for consideration was the school that Kate and Mom attended. It was private and on the expensive side, but they had financial aid packages. I'd probably qualify, given my circumstances. The school offered flexible schedules and the ability to take college courses, either on nearby campuses or online. They had a number of after-school activities as well: dance, music, and culinary arts. Everyone who graduated went on to obtain some form of higher education, which said quite a bit about their program. The school sounded great, but I was somewhat weirded out by the photographs on their website of the wide-smiled, stiffly posed young ladies wearing short white gloves. *Stepford Students. That is so not me.*

I did a quick search of New Orleans schools to see what I could come up with on my own. I found one that sounded really interesting—another charter school with smaller classes where the students could enroll in high school and college classes simultaneously. They offered language immersion classes, which sounded kind of awesome for students who, say, wanted to take their Social Studies class in French, and something called a Transnational Degree Program.

Now that I'd finished my initial research, I could tick that box on my to-do list. I'd check with Kate before I set up tours of each school. She might need to arrange time off from work to take me around. We also needed to discuss money for tuition if necessary. I had no money to speak of. Sam was working on settling my dad's estate. I didn't know what that involved or if there was any money coming to me. Dad never discussed any of this stuff with me. He probably thought I shouldn't be burdened by such things.

Next on my agenda: read up on the place where I'd be doing community service and get familiar with it. After that, I could knock off for a while, have lunch, and then get started with the photo-scanning project. I could definitely stay busy until Kate got home. I found the website for the center where I'd soon be volunteering my time. At-risk teenagers were given an opportunity to learn skills that would help them establish a better direction, a positive career path. These new skills would help them get jobs within the hospitality industry upon graduation. Intrigued by this concept, I searched the Internet further and found a number of on-site interviews with students and graduates. I watched, fascinated, as I learned where and with whom I would soon be spending my time. Their stories were heartfelt, inspiring; they made me a little teary-eyed and somewhat ashamed of my recent reckless behavior.

After finishing the last video, I could easily understand why this was such a personal issue for Kate. She had been blessed by being born into an upper-class white family. She had the opportunity to attend the Culinary Institute of America and work in New York. She had prospered and wanted to give back to her community. And she did. Kate's name was among those listed on the website as guest celebrity chefs who volunteered their time. Something else she hadn't mentioned to me. And now, she had donated my time to them. *But, I had to wonder, what am I supposed to do for them? Chop vegetables, man their restaurant's cash register, mop their floors?* Unquestionably, whatever my responsibilities turned out to be, they would be way better than picking up highway trash or some such nonsense.

Chapter Thirty-Five

I closed my laptop, set it on the table by the chair, and stretched my fingers. They were feeling a little cramped, like the rest of me. I stood at the rail and shook the kinks out, stretching while I watched the people meandering down Royal Street. Cameras and cell phones handy, they were ready to document every little detail of their visit to New Orleans so they could post it on their social media.

My morning had been highly productive. I had a slightly better handle on my own path and was more at peace with my circumstances. I hadn't exactly achieved a "Zen mentality," but I didn't feel nearly as bad about things as I had when I boarded that absurd bus in Montgomery.

My stomach growled. Like yesterday, after researching information for hours and completely losing track of time, I was restless and ready for lunch. I decided to go out and get makeup for tomorrow's interview. I needed to look my best. I found a Saints baseball cap in Kate's office and hoped she wouldn't mind if I borrowed it. I checked on BG, then got my purse and dark glasses and headed up Royal Street. About halfway up the block, I turned around and went back home to call Kate, to leave a voicemail letting her know she shouldn't be concerned if she called and there was no answer. I needed to go out to get makeup for my job interview and would be back in an hour or so.

With that taken care of, I was on my way. It felt good to get out and get some air, even though it was hot and still humid.

I ambled up the sidewalk, stopping along the way to enjoy the window displays of the art galleries and antique shops. A number of shops had cats perched or sleeping in their windows and water dishes on the sidewalks for dogs. *I love that about this place!* Even though I had no clue where to find a store that sold makeup, I knew if I stopped to ask someone, they wouldn't hesitate to help. Folks here seemed pretty easygoing. *Is that why everyone calls New Orleans The Big Easy?*

I wasn't ready to ask for assistance just yet. I wanted to explore on my own, get familiar with my new "hood." I passed by the police station and Café Beignet, finally found a Walgreens and made my purchase. Down the block from the store, a bright red and yellow Lucky Dog cart was open for business. Since Kate had recommended it, I wanted to try one. I slathered my hot dog with yellow mustard, topped it off with a generous helping of relish, and ate it while I explored the famous Bourbon Street. It was crowded, raucous, and claustrophobic—it totally lived up to its reputation for decadence. Strip clubs, jazz joints, sports bars, and souvenir shops selling brightly colored beads, feathered masks, tee shirts, and shot glasses lined both sides of the boulevard. I suspected the street would become even livelier as the day wore on, when the bars and strip clubs were filled beyond capacity and their patrons stumbled out onto the pavement with drinks in hand. I watched as two relaxed, but ready for anything, NOPD mounted officers navigated their steeds through the throng.

I came upon a restaurant Kate had mentioned, Galatoire's. An engraved brass plaque next to the green double doors read *Established in 1905*. The restaurant had maintained its last-century appearance and seemed totally out of place on Bourbon Street. It was beautifully decorated in an old-fashioned way with lace curtains, linen tablecloths, silver flatware, tasteful flower arrangements, and polished brass fixtures. The large dining room was filled with gentlemen in suits, ladies in dresses, and waiters in tuxedos, definitely reminiscent of a bygone era. The restaurant was quite lovely, most certainly a special-occasion restaurant. I lingered in front of the window, envisioning my ghostly grandfather regaling his business companions over a three-martini lunch. For one brief moment, I wished I could join them, to meet the man who'd had such a dramatic impact on my life. When his apparition abruptly faded, I moved on.

I finished my hot dog, elbowed my way through the crowd, and found myself back on Royal Street, behind St. Louis Cathedral, directly in front of a graceful statue of Jesus centered in the garden. I thought about Marie Laveau and how much time she had spent at this cathedral with her friend, Père Antoine. Such an odd pairing, the priest and the high priestess.

I checked my watch. I still had time to wander. I ambled down Pirate's Alley between the St. Louis Cathedral and the Faulkner House Books store and ended up at Jackson Square. The Square pulsated with activity. Fascinated, I watched a rather large man costumed in a massive, brightly hued feathered headdress and loincloth dance for the crowd. He was a Mardi Gras character in need of a float. Nearly every inch of the black wrought iron fence surrounding the park displayed art crafted by local artists. Numerous vendors had set up tables to sell their wares, everything from handmade jewelry and candles to Tarot card and psychic readings. Tourists strolled hand-in-hand soaking up the festive atmosphere.

I bought a soda from a kid with a cart, then sat down on the steps in front of the Cabildo museum and drank it all in. Music was everywhere in the air. Cajun banjo sounds twanged out of the open doors of a nearby restaurant. A saxophone player fingered a bluesy melody over on the far side of the park. A violinist plucked out a vigorous up-tempo piece while wandering amid the mass of sightseers. New Orleans is a living soundtrack. There's an unmistakable energy in this city. Of course, I was completely unaware of it until now; I'd been too wrapped up in my own personal drama to notice. The ancient Cathedral clock rang out the hour. *Time to go.*

I made my way back home through the French Quarter, pleased with myself for not getting lost. I was finally learning my way around. I checked on BG, who was sleeping peacefully on her blanket. Upstairs, I got back to work on Kate's scanning project. Kate had cleared her office floor of the piles of photographs that had already been sorted. I sat down and started over again, dividing everything into piles of color and black-and-white, trying my best to sort according to what appeared to be the logical date sequence, based on cars and clothing.

I didn't recognize anybody until I got to the early years of my mother's childhood and Kate's infancy. In the beginning, the sisters, the cherished Doucet daughters, looked happy. Their precious, priceless moments were frozen for all time. But, as I ordered the years, the girls looked less happy, more forced, more artificial. It made me sad for disrupted childhoods, theirs and mine. If only . . .

I carried on until late in the evening. I was so deep into the project that I didn't hear Kate come in. I jumped at the sound of her voice.

"Sorry, I didn't mean to startle you. It looks like you've made quite a bit of progress."

I stood, rolled my neck and shoulders and arched my back. The floor wasn't all that comfortable for working.

"I didn't hear you come home. Yes, I've made some progress, but not much. I don't know any of the people, except you and Mom. Can you help me after dinner?"

"I'd like that. I brought dinner home from the restaurant. Would you like to try the vegetarian gumbo, maybe have some jambalaya? You do eat seafood, right? Not allergic or anything?"

"I'm good with seafood. I'll go set the table. Wine for you?"

"Not now, maybe later. Let's eat, I'm starving! By the way, I appreciated your voicemail this afternoon. Thanks for letting me know you needed to go out. And congrats on the interview tomorrow!"

Over dinner, I told Kate about the phone pre-interview with Josie. She said if I needed any help to let her know, she'd gone to high school with the owner. I thanked her, but declined her offer. I wanted to get the job on my own. We talked about the three different high schools. Kate agreed it was time to set up tours. She'd get back to me with her availability. Hopefully, we'd knock all of them out in one day and have a nice dinner afterwards. She also said not to worry if tuition was involved, it wouldn't be a problem. *Does Kate mean she'll cover the expenses?* I took her at her word and didn't ask. Kate also said that in between school tours, we would take some time to swing by the facility where I'd be volunteering. She wanted to introduce me to everyone. After I landed a paying job, the supervisor would sort out my non-paying work schedule.

"Finished?" I asked, clearing the dishes.

"I am. Did you like your dinner?"

"Yes. It was really good, not spicy like I thought it would be."

"You can leave those in the sink, I'll get them later," said Kate.

"No, that's all right. You sit, I'll load. After I finish, we'll go through the photos."

"Deal! While you do that, I'll feed BG." Kate hesitated, "By the way, I left a message for the landscaper about our four-legged friend. The assistant manager said the owner would be more than happy to take BG off our hands. She's out of town for a few more days, but he planned to e-mail her tonight and will get back to me with a pick-up date."

I frowned, turned my back on Kate, continued rinsing the dishes and didn't say a word. It would hurt me deeply to see BG leave, even though I knew it was best for her.

Kate lightly squeezed my shoulder. "I'll be sorry to see her go, too; I've grown quite fond of her. But we both know this is her best option. Besides, I haven't given up on the idea of making goat cheese. There'll be ample opportunity for us to keep tabs on our little friend, as well as her new friends. Who knows, if this works out, we could end up with a nice little side business for you and me, making artisan cheeses and selling them to local grocers or at farmer's markets. I could even put our cheeses on the menu! Give it some thought."

I finished the dishes and changed the subject. "Let's go look at the pictures."

Chapter Thirty-Six

Upstairs in Kate's office, we both settled down on the floor, Kate with a glass of wine, me with a bottle of water. While Kate perused the individual stacks of pictures, I explained my process.

"You've done a nice job, April. You've accomplished a lot today. Kudos!" She raised her glass to me and started looking at the pictures individually.

I watched her face as she studied the photographs. I couldn't read Kate at all until she came to the snapshots of her, my mom, and their parents. Scrutinizing each picture, tears and sadness filled her eyes. One by one, she set the family photos aside, stacking them into a tidy little pile.

"Are you okay?" I grabbed the box of tissues off the desk and offered it to her.

Kate removed a tissue and dabbed her eyes. She drank a long swallow of wine before answering.

"Memories, you know? Not always easy. Sometimes better left boxed up."

"Why did you want everything scanned?"

"I don't really know. I guess because it seemed like the right thing to do. After my father died, I felt disconnected and alone."

I could relate.

"Funny thing is, April, I don't recognize most of these people either. I've never looked through these boxes before. I thought when I got around to scanning, I'd know everybody. I just assumed our lives had been well documented up to a certain point . . . I guess I was mistaken."

I picked a photograph out of the pile, held it out to Kate, and said, "Tell me about this day. Where were you and Mom? How old were you? What were you up to? Look at your faces, you were definitely up to something, I can see it."

Kate brightened. She told me about the surprise birthday cake she and my mom had planned to bake all by themselves for their father. A total kitchen disaster followed when she dropped the container of flour and my mother knocked a bowl of fresh eggs off the counter. The cook, Sadie Lee, was mad as a wet hen and banned the two girls from the kitchen for a week.

I handed her another photograph, then another. We continued like that for hours, me giving her photographs, her telling the stories behind them.

"You know, April, this is pretty much the first non-confrontational conversation we've had since you got here."

Embarrassed, I murmured, "I'll be right back" and left the office.

When I returned, Kate's printer was humming with my print job. I grabbed the still warm papers, sat back down, and pulled the photograph of Marie Laveau out of my pocket.

Kate took a sip of wine, looked at the photograph, nodded at the papers, and asked, "What do you have there?"

"I started a family tree. Our tree," I said, pointing to the branches of the tree. "So far, I've added you, me, my parents, my other grandparents, what little I know about your parents, and Marie Laveau. That's as far as I got. Maybe you could help me?"

Kate gaped at me, her face a blank mask.

She finished the last of her wine and stared into the empty glass. "I think a refill might be in order." She left the office and returned a few minutes later with a tray filled with a cheese and fruit plate, a small glass of amber liquid, and more water for me. Kate placed the tray on the floor and settled down across from me.

"What's that?" I pointed to the glass.

"Sherry, it pairs well with the blue cheese, the Brie, and the fruit. Would you like to taste it?"

"No thanks."

Kate took a sip from the delicate crystal glass. "Let's see what we can do, shall we?" she asked, reaching for the papers.

"There's one more thing we should talk about."

"What's that?" asked Kate.

"Angel and Simone."

"Why? What about them?"

"Angel told me that Marie Laveau was her great, great, great, great grandmother. Based on my research of Marie Laveau, I'm pretty sure we're related."

"Your research? . . . Related? . . . How?"

I began, "It all started with the photograph that hangs in Angel's house. It meant nothing at all to me, until I found this one in your box of family pictures. They're identical."

I picked up the photo and handed it to her. Kate didn't say a word, she just sat there. It was impossible to tell what she was thinking.

I continued, tentative but excited. "Of course, we're going to need input from Simone, so we can see if my theory is correct. Though, under the current circumstances, she might not be all that thrilled to hear directly from me."

Kate took another sip of sherry. "Well, well, well, Miss April, you certainly are a never-ending source of surprise . . . You could be right. We all might be related. Everything you said sounds plausible. Tell me, what is your plan for presenting your theory to Simone?"

"I haven't worked that part out yet, I wanted to get your support first . . . You do support me, right?"

"I think I need to sleep on it, April. This could be life changing for all of us," said Kate.

"Would that be a bad thing?" I asked.

"I don't know. Like I said, I need to sleep on it. Let's call it a night."

"'Kay," I mumbled. I was disappointed, but not crushed.

Kate unwound her legs and stood. She picked up the tray, stepped carefully around the piles of pictures, and left the office.

Kate hadn't shot me down, which was good. She also said it was "plausible," which was even better. In fairness, I couldn't be unhappy with her decision to be cautious. Caution had *not* been my strong suit lately. I went to my room to formulate a plan.

I lay down on my bed and over the course of the next hour came up with various alternative scenarios in which I could get Simone to hear me out. None were any good. I got up and went over to the window, stared into the midnight blue, jasmine-scented night, and reversed the roles.

What would I do if someone came to me with this off-the-wall notion of a revised family history? Especially a biracial one? I'd probably freak. Sort of like how I reacted, or overreacted, the night Kate told me that Marie Laveau was my great, great, great, great grandmother. For me, it isn't a race thing, but a Voodoo thing. My great granny, the Voodoo Queen? That's what made me so crazy, sent me spiraling out of control. How would anyone handle that kind of news? Obviously, I didn't handle it well.

Simone might not be all that thrilled with us being related. Not because of the race issue either, but because I'd behaved so badly in recent history. I breathed in the heady perfume of the evening, closed my eyes, and reflected on the situation a while longer. When my brain relaxed, I knew what I had to do. I simply needed to tell the story as I believed it to be.

I had my plan.

Kate would drive me to Simone's house, where first, I would apologize for lying and scaring the daylights out of her by dragging Angel into my misadventure. Second, I would promise to never do anything like that again, although Simone would probably doubt my sincerity. Next, I would apologize to Angel for getting her into such deep doo-doo with her mom.

If Simone were open to listening to me after I begged for forgiveness, I'd tell my tale and try to enlist her help to grow our family tree. I'd already mentioned our kinship to Angel, the night of our hair-raising drive to the swamp. She thought I was crazy. *Maybe I am, but I don't think so.*

The visit might also require peace offerings, some kind of make-nice gifts. I moved over to the comfy chair, pulled up my knees, and ruminated on this new idea for a while. *Will gifts be appropriate or misconstrued?* It could go either way. Ultimately, it would depend upon the gifts being offered. Since this was potentially another touchy situation, I would ask Kate in the morning for her opinion. Gumbo could use a microchip, in case he ever got lost again. The same applied to Angel, but in her case it would be a cell phone with GPS tracking. Any mother would appreciate locators, especially Simone, after what I put her through. I would offer to help pay the phone costs out of my salary if/when I got the job at Café Beignet.

I yawned, stretched, and noted the time. It was already after one in the morning, I needed to call it a night. Tomorrow was going to be a busy day.

Chapter Thirty-Seven

Morning came quickly. I raced downstairs to talk to Kate, to find out what she had decided about bringing all of this to Simone, but she was already gone. There was a note on the fridge wishing me luck on my interview, asking me to call her when I finished. *Well, darn!*

Dejected, I poured myself some orange juice and selected a blueberry muffin from under the glass dome. Before she left, Kate had set a place at the kitchen table for me. Next to the linen napkin was a neatly folded lined piece of paper. I sat down, unfolded the paper and began to read. Sometime during the night or early morning, Kate made notes on the family members she knew about, including full names, dates of births, deaths, marriages, and children whenever possible. There wasn't much, as ours was not a vast family, but whatever information she had, she passed on to me. I interpreted this to mean that she was okay with me/us going to visit Simone and Angel, but wanted me to add more to our side of the family tree before doing so. I was excited, and for the first time in a very long time, happy.

After breakfast, I refilled my juice glass, chopped up some lettuce, and took breakfast out to BG for probably the last time. I released her from the tether, gave her an ear snuggle and watched as she ate the tender greens. I told her not to worry. It wouldn't be much longer before she was spending her days with new friends, free to roam in open spaces. She wouldn't be alone much longer.

When the doorbell sounded, I hooked up BG and went inside. I pulled back the curtain by the door and saw that a delivery man had loaded two large black trunks onto the porch. My belongings had arrived. I opened the door, signed for the delivery, and said he could leave the trunks where they were, I would take care of them. Since I was alone, I didn't want to let a stranger into the house—*Stranger! Danger!* like Detective Baptiste had warned. I went back inside and removed the small rug from the powder room. I slid the first trunk onto it and dragged it across the threshold. I got the second trunk into the house and returned the rug to the powder room. Maybe later, with Kate's help, we could get the trunks upstairs without first unloading everything downstairs.

As I turned to go back to the courtyard, the doorbell sounded again. I pulled the curtain aside. This time it was a FedEx guy with an envelope. I stepped out onto the porch, signed for the letter, went back inside, and locked the front door. The FedEx, sent by Sam, was addressed to me. Outside in the courtyard I sat down and began to read. The documents included a cover letter from Sam, a copy of my father's will, and an envelope addressed to me in my father's handwriting.

Oh boy. This is going to be hard.

I inhaled deeply and began to read Sam's letter. My father's estate was settled. Sam outlined the details in a clear, concise manner. I would have expected nothing less.

I was Dad's sole beneficiary. My father's worldly possessions were stored, along with our furniture, in a facility in Alabama, except for the few personal items that Sam had packed into the trunk for me. He thought I might like to have them right away. *He was right about that.*

I continued reading. I was astonished to learn that I was the sole beneficiary of a life insurance policy that I never knew existed. The proceeds would be administered for me by Sam, as executor of the estate. I was to receive $1,000 per month over the next forty months beginning immediately, until I reached the age of twenty-one. The first $1,000 had already been deposited into my bank account. The balance of the insurance proceeds, in the amount of $160,000, had been set aside for higher education. If for any reason I did not use the $160,000 for college, those funds would not be made available to me until my twenty-fifth birthday. As Dad's will directed, Sam had sold my father's car and would use the money to pay tuition for my last year of high school if necessary. If I attended a public school and tuition was a non-issue, I could use the money to buy a car for myself upon graduation.

Overwhelmed, I began to cry; I sat sobbing in the courtyard for quite some time. When the doorbell rang again, I wiped my face with the hem of my shirt, gathered up all of the papers, and ran inside. Once more, I pulled the curtain aside. Lo and behold, there was yet another delivery person on the porch. A woman this time, holding a small box. I answered the door, signed for the package, and sat down in one of the rocking chairs.

My new phone had arrived. I wasn't in any hurry to activate it, because nobody was going to call me anyway. All I wanted to do was sit here for a while and think about my future. Back and forth, back and forth. Totally drained from this morning's emotional roller coaster, the rocking soothed me; I soon drifted off.

Somewhere up the street a car backfired and I awoke with a start. I checked my watch and panicked. My job interview was in thirty-five minutes. I snatched up the box with the phone, took the stairs two at a time and speed-showered. I pulled back my hair, bound it with a clip, found the makeup I'd purchased the day before, and went about the business of hiding the nearly healed scratches on my face. I threw on a long-sleeved white shirt, plain black trousers, and black sandals, added a pair of simple gold hoop earrings, and finished off with a little bit of pink lip gloss.

I grabbed my purse, locked the front door, and flew down the porch stairs, happy the interview was only a few short blocks away.

I fast-walked up Royal Street, then had to slow my pace a bit so I wouldn't be all sweaty and overheated when I arrived at Café Beignet. I felt a pang when I passed in front of the police station. I thought about the night I met Miles and the conversation we had, when he joked that he hoped I was worth all the bother. Because I hadn't heard from him since my swamp incident, I assumed I wasn't.

The truth hurt.

I pushed the dark, brooding thoughts out of my head, pulled out a smile from somewhere deep within, entered the café and looked for Josie, the manager. Right away I recognized the infectious laughter from our initial phone call, but Josie would have been hard to miss. She was wearing a brightly colored oversized Hawaiian shirt with huge hibiscus flowers blooming across her substantial chest. There was a real hibiscus flower holding back the hair above her left ear, and on each wrist she wore numerous gold bangle bracelets, which jingled with every laugh. She looked like a lady that dotted the 'i' in Josie with a little flower. I liked her immediately.

Josie came around to the front of the counter, reached out her hand, and said, "Hi, I'm Josie. You must be April."

"How did you know?"

"Your outfit, it's very interview-ish. You look quite professional, entrepreneurial, as well as gorgeous, and you're five minutes early. I like you already! Let's sit, you can tell me all about yourself. Can I get you a café au lait before we start?"

"Maybe after. Thank you for asking. I would like some water, though."

"Polite, too, I like that in an employee," said Josie, handing me a frosty glass of water.

Josie sat. We visited, laughed, and got to know each other over the next hour. I'd never been on a job interview before, but Josie made it easy. I was comfortable with her; I felt as if I were speaking with a kindred spirit.

In one quick move, Josie rose from her chair, squeezed my shoulder and said, "Let me get that café au lait for you now, sugar." The interview was over. *I didn't get the job!* The opportunity had slipped away and I didn't understand why. I failed miserably. *Now what am I going to do? I need to start the job hunt all over again to satisfy Kate's conditions for my continued presence in her home. And I won't get to see Miles.* I wanted to cry, but didn't. It had already been a teary kind of day.

Josie returned to the table with two coffees and a plate of freshly made beignets. She sat back down.

"Let's celebrate!"

"Celebrate what?"

"Why, honey, your new job, of course. When can you start? Monday morning okay with you?"

"I'm hired? Really? Wow! Thank you!" I raised my coffee cup in a toast to Josie, took a bite of beignet and unleashed the power of powdered sugar.

"You might want to re-think wearing black to work, hon," laughed Josie.

I finished my food, stood, stacked the dishes, cleared the table, and carried everything into the kitchen. Before leaving the kitchen, I washed my hands at the employee sink and wiped the powdered sugar from my trousers with a damp paper towel.

I reached out my hand to Josie and said, "I want to thank you for your time today and for giving me this opportunity. You won't regret it."

"Of that, I have no doubt. I'll see you here on Monday at ten A.M. We'll work out the rest of your schedule later."

"Yes, ma'am! I'll be here bright and early," I said, throwing her a little salute.

Turning to leave, I collided with Detective Baptiste.

"What's your hurry, little lady?" he asked.

"Um . . . hi . . . uh, hello . . . Detective Baptiste."

"You two know each other?" asked Josie.

"We're old friends. We just haven't seen each other for a while. Right, April?" he answered.

"That's right. Old friends," I croaked, surprised I could get the words out of my desert-dry mouth.

"The usual?" asked Josie.

"Yep, the usual. I'll just sit here and catch up with Miss April while I wait," he said, pulling a chair away from the table for me.

Speechless, I sat.

"How are you, April? How's Kate?"

"I'm better. She's better. I mean, *we're* doing better. Together."

Detective Baptiste listened quietly, patiently.

I rambled on, "We're working on our, uh, hmmm . . . issues, I guess you could call it."

"Glad to hear it. I was concerned." Detective Baptiste leaned closer to me and lowered his voice. "You seem to be a pretty good kid, April, but you're a little feisty and maybe a tad too reckless. I would hate to see you get hurt."

I looked down at the table, embarrassed, "Thank you for your concern, for everything. You were a big help to me . . . to us. I know Kate really appreciated—I mean appreciates—you. She likes you a lot . . . a whole lot . . . she says you're a good man and a kind person."

"You mean she didn't say anything about my ruggedly handsome face, exquisite manners, or musical talent?" he laughed.

I laughed, too; it felt good, natural. It was a relief.

Josie brought his "usual" to the table and asked, "So Frank, what do you think of my new hire?"

"With her charm, she'll fit right in here. Most likely, she'll increase your business, too. Especially the male NOPD rookie business."

"Mighty fine," she said, dancing her way back to the counter to help the new customers, "mighty fine . . ."

"Um, Detective Baptiste . . . how's Miles?"

He smiled at me and nodded towards the door. "Why don't you ask him yourself?"

Chapter Thirty-Eight

There, leaning against the door frame, bathed in the golden late-afternoon sun, was Miles. With his tanned, muscular arms folded across his six-pack abs, he looked better than ever. He also looked like a panther assessing its prey. My heart skipped a beat; I couldn't breathe or think clearly.

Detective Baptiste stood. "It was nice seeing you again, April. I'm happy to hear that you're doing so well." He leaned down, gave me a little peck on the cheek and whispered, "Don't be afraid, he won't bite."

"Son."

"Dad."

Miles strode over to the table; he took me by the arm and led me towards the exit.

"Let's take a walk."

I glanced back at Josie and waved goodbye.

She winked, gave me two thumbs up and mouthed, "You go, girl!"

Miles waited until we were well out of sight of the café and the police station, before turning me towards him and gently backing me up against a brick wall. I wasn't afraid, but I didn't know what to expect.

It certainly wasn't what happened next.

Miles cupped my chin and planted a long, hard kiss on my lips.

"Why haven't you returned my texts or voicemails ? I've been worried sick. Are you angry with me, April?"

Breathless, I was grateful the wall was holding me up. I enjoyed his closeness, his warmth, the lingering taste of his kiss still fresh on my mouth.

"What? What are you talking about? Angry with you? Are you kidding me? I thought you were mad at me for all the trouble I caused. I thought I'd never see you again!"

Miles peered down at the sidewalk. "Well, yeah, I *was* angry with you. To be honest, I never wanted to see you again. After Dad talked to me about what you said in your statement, I felt bad. I felt bad for you. And for me. I was awfully hurt because you wouldn't talk to me about yourself. I thought we were friends. What I really couldn't understand was why you didn't answer any of my texts. I must've sent a gazillion of them before I took the hint."

"The hint? *There was no hint!* My phone is deep in the swamp; it's probably gator food by now. I just got my replacement phone this morning. I haven't even had time to activate it."

"Really?"

"Really!"

"So, we're good?"

"We're more than good." I turned my face upwards and puckered my lips, ready for another kiss.

The kiss didn't come. Instead Miles joked, "I don't suppose you'd like to join me tonight for a cemetery tour and a visit to the Voodoo shop?"

At first I was taken aback. Then I laughed. I laughed long and hard.

"Been there, done that."

"May I walk you home?"

"I'd like that very much."

Miles hooked his arm in mine and turned me towards home. *Home. I guess it is my home now, isn't it?*

Arriving at the front gate, Miles offered to help me with the phone. I declined his offer and let him know I wanted to handle it myself, that I'd call or text later.

I needed some alone time. This day had been so much more than I could have imagined when I went to bed last night. My life was happening at warp speed and I was having difficulty keeping up.

I sat in the rocker and watched Miles walk away from the gate. He really was quite a remarkable person, just like his dad. They were both good, kind men. Never in a million years would I have believed we would be friends again. I thought about what Miles said to me earlier about our friendship. If he hadn't been so discouraging about Voodoo in the beginning, I might have opened myself up to him, but then again, maybe not. At the time, I really wasn't in a frame of mind to open up to anyone. I hoped I could do better going forward.

I rocked awhile longer, trying to decide when I would open my father's letter. I wanted to read it, but not yet. I was still aching from his death, his permanent absence. I knew the contents would make me cry. In my heart, I knew he was going to tell me to let him go. I wasn't ready to hear it. I'd seen it too many times in the movies: *"If you're reading this, I must be dead . . ."* It had to be one of those letters.

His letter could wait. I rocked some more and thought about Kate, Simone, Angel. I thought about high school and college and money and volunteering and my new job. By the time I finished, my head was spinning. I needed food. Since I hadn't eaten anything except a muffin and a beignet, I was once again on sugar overload. I got up, unlocked the front door, and saw the trunks that had been delivered earlier in the day. The trunks could wait.

Leaving my keys and handbag on the hall table, I moved past the trunks and into the kitchen to fix myself something to eat.

Kate's note from the morning was still hanging on the fridge. *Oh my God! I was supposed to call her after my interview!* I picked up the receiver and dialed, hung up when I heard the front door open. Kate was home.

She entered the kitchen and slipped her carry-all over the back of a chair, then kicked off her shoes, sat down at the kitchen table, and began to rub her ankles.

"Tough day?"

"Not really. My feet are a bit sore, that's all. How was your day? How did your interview go? By the way, you look really nice. Very professional."

"I apologize for not calling you, I got sort of distracted. My day was good, the interview went really well. I got the job! I start Monday."

"That's great news! Congratulations! We should celebrate. We could go anywhere, do anything you like. Would you be interested in a jazz dinner cruise on the Mississippi? The buffet isn't five-star, but the food is good and there's plenty of it. It's touristy, but interesting and fun. We wouldn't need to be there until close to seven P.M., so you have time to decide. I saw your trunks in the hall. Would you like help getting them upstairs?"

"Thanks, I could use your help. And a river cruise sounds like fun. We haven't had much of that lately. Actually, we haven't had any fun since I arrived in New Orleans which, I know, is totally my fault . . . Let's do it!"

Kate eyed the FedEx on the kitchen table, "What's that?"

"It's from Sam. Dad's estate is settled. Sam sent me the details. We can talk about it over dinner."

Kate stood. "Let's get those trunks upstairs."

It was a struggle, but we got them into the hallway outside my room. I could unpack from there and store the trunks in the attic afterwards. Unpacking could wait.

I was ready to go out and have some fun.

Chapter Thirty-Nine

The pier was packed with people ready to experience the local color of Louisiana. Nothing says vacation in New Orleans like a steam-powered riverboat ride on the Mississippi, with an endless buffet of Creole delicacies, oversized alcoholic beverages, and an overlay of jazz in the background. The energy was contagious. I was as excited as the tourists.

The evening air was cooler by the river. It was a welcome relief, and it got even cooler once the trip was under way. We worked our way through the crowd to the front of the boat to get the best view. When we found a comfortable space at the railing, we relaxed and enjoyed the scenery. We passed factories, antebellum homes, an old fort, and a plantation. Our fellow passengers were loud, but in a background, white-noise way.

After twenty minutes of cruising down the muddy Mississippi, I told Kate about my day. I started with the morning deliveries, worked my way up to the afternoon interview, my chance meeting with Detective Baptiste, the walk with Miles. I left out his kiss, which was way too private. I ended with the details of the estate settlement and the as-yet unopened letter from my dad.

Kate was a good listener. Not once did she interrupt.

The dinner bell sounded; it was time for the first seating. I was famished. Inside, we gave our dinner tickets to the steward who, with a flirty little wink at Kate, led us to a nice table by the window.

He took our drink order, pointed to the stack of plates at the buffet, and said, "Help yourselves, beautiful ladies. I'll be right back with your beverages."

It was indelicate of me, but I pretty much piled one of everything from the buffet onto my plate before returning to the table. Kate's plate was overloaded as well. Over in the corner, on a small, raised stage, the jazz quartet played mellow music during our meal. In between mouthfuls, I talked about school, about money, about our new extended family. After dessert, I lay down my fork and finally talked about my dad.

Until I said it out loud to Kate, I hadn't realized the depth of my anger with my dad for dying. For leaving me alone, without support, either emotional or financial. I'd been pissed off beyond all reason every day since he died. It was fairly obvious that, to date, I hadn't handled myself very well. To make matters worse, I'd been wrong about everything. My dad did have a plan in case of emergency, he just ran out of time before he could tell me.

When I finished, Kate said, "Thank you."

"For what?"

"For helping me understand you a little better."

"Does this mean I don't have to go to grief counseling?"

Kate rolled her eyes, "Let's just say you've made great progress tonight . . . Listen, while we're clearing the air, are you okay if I talk about your mother now? I think I can help you understand her a little better."

I hesitated before answering. "Okay."

"Dad used to think Julia was something special. He always said she was like lightning in a bottle, impossible to contain. He had great aspirations for her, wanted her to be a lawyer, follow in his and Grandpa's footsteps by taking over the firm one day."

It was my turn to be a good listener, but hearing this stuff wasn't easy for me. It was work to be still and focused.

"When Julia got pregnant with you, she was trapped. Since abortion was out of the question, Mom hid her in a home for unwed mothers and told their friends she was spending time abroad studying at the Cordon Bleu. Which, by the way, had always been *my* dream. Our parents wanted her to give you up for adoption. They actually considered you to be nothing more than a minor impediment to the future they had mapped out for their precious daughter. Life at home became unbearable, the arguments were frequent and bitter. Julia wanted to keep you. In her mind, adoption was out of the question. Finally, against our father's wishes, Mom brought both of you back from the home for unwed mothers and kept you hidden from public view while she tried to sort things out. Dad was adamant, you had to go. It wasn't long before Julia left everything and everyone behind."

Wrapping my arms around myself, I stared at her, unblinking, holding back any tears.

Kate continued, "Julia was miserable, frightened. She couldn't keep you and raise you on her own. She wouldn't give you up to strangers. On the morning of her eighteenth birthday, she did the only thing she could think to do. She got up at dawn, put you in the pram, left you on your father's front porch and disappeared. It wasn't until later we learned she'd joined the Army. That's when our parents went to her room, removed all evidence of her, gave her clothes to charity, and stored the rest of her things in a trunk tucked away in the attic." Kate took a deep breath and a sip of water.

"Go on."

"It all went downhill from there. Our parents went their separate ways. Not literally of course, they stayed together for appearances' sake. My father became a huge fan of daily three-martini lunches. My mother gave endless afternoon card parties, serving her guests large pitchers of icy cold mint juleps. They both began to smoke. They both embraced vices they had previously looked upon with disdain."

"And you?"

"Me? I developed good coping skills. I never complained, I kept to myself, kept my distance. Most important of all, I held on to my dream. I never made it to the Cordon Bleu, but graduated from the Culinary Institute of America instead. I stayed in New York after graduation and worked my way up in high-end restaurants until Dad died."

"Are you still angry with my mom?" I asked.

"I was. But you changed that for me."

"How?"

"By helping me understand that by leaving you with your father, she gave you a better start in life. As difficult as it was, she did what she thought was best for you. Turns out she was right."

The dinner bell rang once more, it was time for the second seating and they needed our table. Kate and I resumed our positions at the front of the boat.

We talked until we docked. By the end of the cruise, Kate had approved of my idea to have Gumbo microchipped and to pre-pay a cell phone for Angel. She said if I could get the balance of our family tree finished either tonight or in the morning, we'd go see Simone and Angel after her shift ended tomorrow afternoon.

It had been a good day—more than good, actually—but I was worn out and ready to go home.

"I don't feel like walking home," said Kate. "If we get a carriage, the driver can let us out in front of the house."

"You read my mind."

We ambled over to the first carriage, made our request of the driver, and climbed in. Soon Kate dozed off, with her head on my shoulder, snoring softly.

The carriage driver pulled to a stop at our gate, bid us good night, and rolled away into the darkness, searching for his next fare. I locked up the house while Kate went upstairs to bed. It was time for me to do the same.

Before bed, I booted up my laptop and checked my e-mail. There was one from Sam with the combination for the trunk locks. I went back into the hallway and opened the trunks. The first trunk held the rest of my clothes. The second trunk contained the balance of my belongings, as well as my father's personal mementos. A jewelry box, two framed photographs, and two small blue leather photo albums were neatly tucked away in a corner. I removed my father's things and left all of my stuff for another time. There was no rush to unpack. I wasn't going anywhere.

I closed the trunks and brought his things into my room. One silver-framed photograph was of me and my dad, taken on my birthday last year. I immediately placed it on the dresser. The second photograph was one I'd never seen before, of my mother and father dressed in formal attire. *Junior prom?* I set it aside. The first photo album was older, yellow with age. I flipped page after page, fascinated as my dad's and some of my mom's life, from elementary to high school, unfolded before me. The pictures stopped at about age seventeen. I never knew he had these pictures or an album of himself and my mother. I guess it was too personal and too painful to share with me.

The second album began with baby pictures of me and continued until Dad's birthday party, taken not long before he died. I set both albums aside, opened the lid of the brown leather jewelry box, and began to empty the contents. Dad had never worn much jewelry. He had a sports watch, a daytime watch with a black leather strap, and a beautiful gold special-occasion watch. They were all inside.

I removed the gold watch, clasped it to my wrist, and admired it. It was a little too big, but it looked good, and it made me feel good; it made me feel close to him.

There were three pairs of antique gold cufflinks, which had belonged to his father. It was nice that Dad kept them, even though I'd never seen him wear a shirt with French cuffs. I wondered if they could be made into earrings.

Nestled inside a gold-trimmed red leather box was a gold Cartier ballpoint pen. I remembered the day he bought it.

He said, "It makes me feel important to have one good writing instrument. Everyone should own at least one."

Now I did.

I was ready now. I got up and placed the photo albums, prom picture, and jewelry box on the dresser. I retrieved his letter, settled into my comfy chair, took a deep breath, and began to read his final words to me.

My Dearest Daughter,

There is so much I would like to say to you, but don't know how. Obviously, if you are reading this, something unforeseen has happened to me that neither one of us is prepared for.

I did what I could to provide for your future. Sam will give you the details when everything is settled. You will have some financial stability, but not as much as I would have liked. For that I apologize. I wish I could have done better for you.

You are the best daughter a father could ever hope for. You are sweet, kind, smart, funny, and courageous. You are, and always have been, the most precious gift.

As you make your way in life, please do not base your decisions on what you think I would want you to do. Base your decisions on what you believe will be in your best interest.

The best life recommendations I can give you would be the following:

#1 Be Self Loving
#2 Pursue Your Passion
#3 Follow Your Heart
#4 Trust Your Instincts

> *Please be kind to Kate. You don't understand it yet, but you need her in your life. I know you are feeling terribly alone. Remember that you aren't. You have family and you will make new friends.*
>
> *Your mother may come back into your life one day and, if she does, I hope you will be able to show her your compassion instead of your anger. Be the kind-hearted person I know you to be.*
>
> *At some point in a letter like this, I should probably advise you to let me go. I should tell you to get on with your life. But, knowing you the way I do, you will do that only when you are ready. For your sake, I hope it is sooner rather than later, as prolonged despair can only hurt you.*
>
> *There is so much joy ahead for you in life, even though you feel no joy today. Know that I am, and always will be, here as your guardian angel, your spirit-guide. I'm sure this brings you little or no comfort in your time of grief. Maybe it even sounds a bit lame. But hey, what do you expect? I'm your dad, and dads are traditionally lame.*
>
> *I will miss you, my sweet April!*
>
> Love always and always watching,
>
> Dad

It was such a beautiful letter, so typical of Dad. Short, to the point, no wasted words or sentiments. It was precisely what I needed from him. I tucked the letter back inside the envelope, slid it under my pillow, crawled beneath the sheet, and fell into a deep, peaceful sleep.

Chapter Forty

I awoke refreshed and ready to get started. I wanted to bring the family tree as close to completion as possible with our information, so we could go visit Simone and Angel later today. I missed my little friend. I hoped her mother wouldn't turn me away. I didn't have many friends and not much family. It was important to me to do this, to bring us all together. I hoped everyone else agreed.

I found Kate bustling in the kitchen, fresh cookies cooling on the counter and a pink bakery box waiting to be loaded.

"Wow! How long have you been up?"

"Not long. I keep cookie dough in the freezer for emergencies. I thought we could take a box with us today, a part of our peace offering."

"Um, uh . . . I don't think that's such a good idea."

"Why not?"

When I came clean about using a box of her baked goods as subterfuge for visiting Simone and absconding with Angel into the swamp, Kate stopped what she was doing and put the box back in the butler's pantry.

Frustrated, she turned to me. "Have you always been this way?"

"What way?"

"Challenging. You've been more than difficult ever since you stepped off the bus. I'd like to know if you've always been this way or if it's just a part of your grieving process."

I hesitated, "Well, I must admit, my actions have been a little over the top since I got here, but the short answer is *No*. I was a good girl with an ordinary life."

"Good to know," said Kate, as she pulled another sheet of cookies from the oven. "I can drop these off at the police station for Detective Baptiste and the boys in blue before we go to see Angel and Simone."

"Shouldn't you be at work?"

"I'm off today. I traded shifts so we could do this. While you finish your work on the family tree, I'll take care of the cell phone for Angel and pick up a gift certificate for microchipping Gumbo. By the way, the landscape company owner is back from vacation. She wants to pick up BG as soon as possible."

"Darn. I love that little goat. I'll miss her."

"Me too . . . Hungry?"

"Not really. I think I'll just take some juice and yogurt upstairs and get to work on the tree. I also need to activate my phone."

"Let me know if you need anything."

Upstairs, I took care of the phone first, sent Miles a *Good morning!* text and got to work. I logged into my Ancestry.com account and was surprised to see leaves with new hints. I read through the hints, saved the pertinent ones to my shoebox. I began to add the family details Kate provided. Though the tree was far from complete, I was making progress. I could easily understand how people could lose themselves evaluating information; the census records, the birth/death/marriage records—it's all there to be researched. Everyone's lives are well documented, now more than ever with social media. I sat back and admired my work in progress.

If my assumptions were correct, my mother's side of the family descended from Marie Laveau's illegitimate daughter, Delphine, who had been raised as white and had married a wealthy white man. I believed Angel's side of the family descended from Delphine's daughter, Liga, the very dark skinned baby who was raised by her grandmother, Marie Laveau. I wouldn't actually know if my logic was sound until we saw Simone. I had done as much as I could do alone.

I was ready to make my presentation.

I printed the family tree and got up to get my laptop case. I opened the armoire and saw that Marguerite's Voodoo doll had fallen out of her gift bag. The sightless button eyes stared at me, but I was no longer frightened. This little piece of herb-filled fabric had led me on my journey, to a new beginning, to my new family. I set the Voodoo doll on my dresser. It belonged there, right next to the photograph of Marie Laveau.

I packed up my laptop, the charger, and the hard copy of the family tree and went downstairs to wait for Kate, but she was already home. After dropping the cookies at the police station, she had picked up the gift certificate for the vet and purchased the phone for Angel.

"Ready?" she asked.

"Ready."

The day was spectacularly beautiful and we drove with the top down. The traffic was light; it didn't take long to get to Simone's house.

The house looked different, better. New front steps had been installed, a new railing surrounded the porch, and half of the house was covered in fresh paint. A concrete mixer sat next to their broken sidewalk and new shingles were stacked nearby. Last but not least, there was a pink bicycle propped up by the newly screened front door.

Angel flew out of the door, with Gumbo loping behind. Simone stood in the doorway. I couldn't read her expression.

"You came, you came! I thought I'd never see you again!" She threw herself at me, her hug nearly squeezing all breath out of me. Angel pointed at her house. "Look what your boyfriend and his friends did for us! He got a bike for me! He said he traded with a neighbor for work they needed done. You oughta hang on to him!"

"I'll do my best."

Simone opened the screen door and came out onto the porch. She looked none too happy, "Why are you here?"

"I came to apologize to you. And to Angel. I came to say I'm sorry for deceiving you, for putting Angel in harm's way. None of what happened was her fault. I'd like to make amends. I need to make this right."

"Last time you came, you lied to me and you lied to my Angel. You took her away and filled her head with stuff about us bein' cousins. That wasn't right, not right at all. Now go on, go away!"

"Okay, I'll go. But, first, would you please take a look at this?"

I handed her the copy of the family tree. Neither Kate nor Angel spoke. Neither one wanted any part of our exchange.

"Five minutes. You get five minutes. Come sit while I look at it."

Five minutes, then ten, then fifteen minutes passed. The silence was profound. Simone set down the printout, got up and went inside. She returned less than a minute later, carrying a well-worn black book, which she handed to me.

"Open it."

On the cover, stamped in flaking gold letters, was *HOLY BIBLE*. I opened the fragile leather tome and gasped. Inside the cover was a fading, handwritten family tree. This was Simone's family Bible, passed down through generations. I traced my finger lightly over the discolored parchment. Listed at the top of the tree, in bright blue ink, was Angelique (Angel) Lacroix, next in line was Simone Lacroix. No father had been entered for Angel, no husband for Simone. I read through the scrawled, barely legible, faded names and dates until I reached the beginning of the tree: *Liga Laveau, daughter of Delphine, grand-daughter of Marie.*

I was at a total loss for words. I handed the Bible to Kate and gaped at Simone.

"I guess we're never gonna get rid of you now. You're family!" Simone turned to Angel, "Baby, go set two more places for lunch."

I gave Simone a bear hug and said, "Thank you. Thank you, Cousin Simone, for helping bring us all together!"

"Oh, Lord, what've I gotten us into?"

Simone and Kate stayed on the porch and visited, while Angel and I set the table and got lunch ready. We had lots of food and lots to talk about. None of us knew where this new information, this new family, would take us, but we knew it would take us there together. Simone was right. There's no gettin' rid of me now.

Kate and I stayed long into the evening. Kate helped Angel and Simone with the new phone. Gumbo slept at my feet. I booted up the laptop, but couldn't get into my Ancestry.com account since there was no Wi-Fi. *Note to self: need a plan for a computer and Internet service for Angel.* I grabbed a pen and paper and began to takes notes from the details in Simone's Bible. I'd add them on Ancestry.com later.

We still had loads of questions, some of which may never be answered. Not all of our history was recorded, at least not that I had found yet. I planned to keep digging into our roots. I needed to expand my father's side of the family and Angel's if Simone was up to sharing her secrets. It was after midnight when Kate and I bid our good nights and headed back to the French Quarter. We didn't speak on the drive home, but it was an easy silence. We'd had a long, exhausting, wonderful day and were too tired to talk.

As Kate pulled in front of the house, my phone alerted to an incoming text. Miles wanted to come by to see me tomorrow afternoon. I texted back an enthusiastic *YES!*

"You did an amazing thing for us, April. I couldn't be more proud of you."

"Aunt Kate?"

"Yes?"

"Thanks for not giving up on me."

Chapter Forty-One

When the doorbell rang, I ran to get it, hoping Miles was early. I fluffed my curls, checked my face in the mirror above the hall table, put on a huge smile and flung open the door.

Marguerite stood before me holding a beautifully wrapped package in her hands. My smile instantly vanished.

Tense as a coiled rattlesnake, I blurted, "You! What are you doing here? How did you find me?"

"No magic in finding you. Your auntie is listed in the phone book. She should change that, you know. There are lots of dangerous people in the world."

"Go away! You're not welcome here!"

"I won't be long. May we talk? Just a few minutes of your time?"

"Five minutes. You get five minutes." I pointed to the rockers. "Over there. Pardon me if I don't offer you any chamomile tea or tea cakes. I'm feeling less than hospitable."

We sat. She began.

"April, I want you to know how sorry I am. I meant you no harm. You weren't ready for a Voodoo ceremony. I know that now. When you came to me, you were desperate to contact your father. I thought the ceremony would be beneficial, that it would help you find the closure you sought. If you believed your father's spirit was finally at peace, you could get on with your life."

"Animal sacrifice? That would help me move on? How was that supposed to work?"

"*Chère*, the sacrifice of animals is part of our ritual, part of our culture; it is a way of life that has always been. However, in *my* ceremonies, the animals are symbolic. They are *never* killed. My business could not withstand any retribution by animal rights activists. And the children and grandchildren of the devotees would never forgive them if they harmed an animal. There are those who still practice the old ways, but the animals are consumed afterwards, they do not go to waste. It really is no different from what happens to animals on a farm or deer in the forest or ducks in the sky."

"That's supposed to make me feel better? You're not really helping yourself out here, Madame."

"I need not justify my beliefs. I came here only to apologize for what happened and to bring this to you. A peace offering." She handed me the beautiful box.

"What is it?"

"A simple token, nothing more." She stood, ready to go. "My five minutes are up. I shall leave you in peace."

"*Bleat! Bleat!*"

Marguerite stopped; she smiled at me enigmatically, just as she had that night in the swamp, then she quickly descended the stairs.

"Marguerite, wait!" I faltered, "Thank you . . . Thank you for . . . your gift."

Marguerite turned back around and for the last time, her pale gold gaze fell on me.

"You are most welcome, my child."

Miles brushed past Marguerite on his way in the gate. He bounded up the steps and gave me a questioning look.

"But Dad warned . . ."

"Miles, she's gone now. For good."

He pointed at the package. "What's that?"

"She said it was a token."

"Are you going to keep it?"

"Depends on what it is."

"Aren't you going to open it?"

"Not now."

"Aren't you curious?"

"Only about how we're going to spend the day."

I yawned and stretched lazily. Miles took the rocker next to me.

"I could take you on a tour of the plantations. That would be fun."

"Naw, no tours for a while. The cemetery and Voodoo tour was enough to last me for maybe the rest of my life!"

"How about some lunch? Now there's a good idea. We could go to Coop's for fried chicken. They have the best in N'awlins."

I stared at Miles, horrified. "I'm kind of off chicken these days . . ."

"Yeah, right. Makes sense," he said.

"Is there somewhere we could get something vegetarian?"

"Are you kidding? In this town? Where can't we get great food? Even vegetables." Miles rose, bowed and held out his hand, "Shall we go?"

I took his hand.

"How about we pick up a couple of Muffulettas and some sweet tea? We can sit by the river and watch the paddle wheelers steam by."

"What's a Muffuletta?"

"You want the long or the short answer?"

"I know you're just *aching* to impart some of your vast knowledge, so I'll take the long answer!"

Miles began, "The first Muffuletta was created at the Central Grocery, near the French Market. Sicilian farmers who were selling their goods at the Market used to come to the grocery for their salami, ham, cheese, olive salad, and bread. They'd all sit around on crates or barrels and have their lunch before going back to work. It was kind of hard to eat that way because they ate everything separately. One day, the grocery store owner, Mr. Salvatore Lupo, suggested putting the salami, ham, cheese, and olive salad in between the round loaf of bread, which is called Muffuletta and, voilà, the Muffuletta sandwich was born."

"Do they make vegetarian ones?"

"Indeed they do!"

"Let's do it!"

We made our way towards the Central Grocery in companionable silence. Miles stopped, took my hands and pulled me into him.

"You know, April, we've never discussed where we're going."

My breath caught, my heart raced.

"I thought we were going to get something to eat. Aren't we?" I asked in my most innocent of voices.

"That's not what I meant and you know it. I meant you and me. Us. Where are WE going?"

I stammered, "Uh . . . I . . . uh, don't really know. Is there an us?"

"You tell me, April. Is there an us?" he asked, his breath warming my skin. "You know there's only one way to keep all of those pretty little Tulane co-eds away from me, right?"

"How?" I murmured, turning my lips upward towards his, closing my eyes in anticipation.

"You!" He leaned down, gently kissed my forehead, my cheeks, my nose and, at long last, my lips.

I wrapped my arms around Miles, melted into the moment, hoping it would last forever.

Miles lightly pushed me back and laughed. "There! That should give you something to think about." He grinned, tightened his arm around my waist, "Now, let's get something to eat."

We claimed an unoccupied bench by the river's edge and spread out our feast. I took one bite of the massive sandwich and said, "Thank you, Mr. Lupo! This bread with the olive salad is awesome!"

We ate in silence, watching the paddle wheeler, *Queen of the Mississippi*, move slowly past us, its music and laughter floating lightly over the murky river. There was a nice breeze and it was lovely here by the water. I leaned over, rested my head on Miles's shoulder, closed my eyes, and enjoyed the respite from the heat. I wondered if this might be the beginning of my new normal.

Miles grinned, "So, Miss April, how do you like New Orleans so far?"

I smiled, "Not bad. A little boring for my taste. Seems like nothing much exciting ever happens here in *The Big Easy*. A little too *Smallville*, don't you think?"

Miles laughed. "In a Quentin Tarantino kind of way."

"Exactly!"

Miles gently kissed my curls, making me vibrate. "Ready to go?"

"I am."

At our front gate, Miles leaned down and kissed me once more. "Kissing you could become a habit."

"I'm a hard habit to break."

I closed the gate behind him and floated up the sidewalk to the porch. Kate was out with her girlfriends for the evening. I had the house to myself. I thought about my afternoon with Miles and smiled as I climbed the stairs. I crawled into bed, tucked my legs under me, and tuned the radio to a smooth jazz station. I laughed out loud when I heard the announcer say in his deep, raspy late-night voice, "For all you lovebirds out there listening tonight, coming up for one uninterrupted hour, *Love Songs* by Miles Davis." *Perfect, just perfect!*

Sinking back on the pillows, I closed my eyes and breathed in the heady floral scent of magnolia drifting in with the breeze. When I remembered Marguerite's gift, I bolted from the room, ran back down the stairs, snatched the package off the table and brought it back to my room. It was heavy; I hoped it wasn't another How-to-Voodoo book. I dropped the gift box at the end of the bed and lay back on the pillows, studying the package as if it were a beautifully wrapped bomb.

Completely agitated, I sat up and reached for it. I couldn't just leave it there, like an unfinished thought. I undid the ribbon and threw it aside. I slid my finger down the seam and released the package from the beautiful paper. I examined the box. There was nothing to indicate what the contents were. I set it down again and paced the room. Finally, I gathered up what was left in my reservoir of courage and opened the box.

"Oh-my-God-oh-my-God-oh-my-God! Not again."

Another scented vellum envelope fixed with Marguerite's signature red wax seal lay on top of the tissue paper. I tore open the envelope and withdrew her letter:

My dear, lovely, April,

You are kind, considerate, intelligent, but above all else, you are courageous.

You are the product of a rich, vibrant past.

You have the potential for a rich, vibrant future.

Yours is a story worth telling.

Your life from this day on is a blank book. How you fill the pages is up to you.

May your journey be a blessed one!

Your friend
Marguerite

I opened the tissue and removed a beautiful black leather journal. *April Lockhart* was embossed in gold, with a gold fleur-de-lis centered directly underneath. I ran my hand over the fine-grained leather. It was cool and had a nice feel to it. I held it to my nose. It smelled expensive, rich, like my family history. I believed Marguerite was right. My family's saga would make great narrative. I settled back on the pillows, opened the book, and fanned the blank pages. After a while, I put the journal aside, closed my eyes and nodded off. An idea bounced into my brain. I got back out of bed, gathered up my father's gold pen, picked up my new journal, and dropped into my comfy chair. The new leather was stiff; it creaked when I opened it. On the first blank page, I wrote, *Color Blind, Chapter One*. It wasn't much, but it was a start.

Every story had to start somewhere.

I closed the cover, leaned back in the chair. In that moment, I knew I would write this book. I got up, placed my journal on top of the dresser, and laid the gold pen beside it. It was my gold pen now and I would cherish it forever. The antique dresser, which had been passed down through generations, was newly populated with an assortment of framed extended family photos: my dad and me, my parents at the prom, Marie Laveau, and the "selfie" of me, Kate, Angel, and Simone holding the family Bible. And, of course, the little button-eyed Voodoo doll, which had started the journey for me, now held a place of honor with the rest of the family.

That night, I made a promise to myself: no matter how long it took, I would write our story. I climbed back into bed, turned off the light, and drifted off listening to the romantic sounds of smooth jazz playing on the radio.